Olivia Drew 

The Light Witch

To Pat Gillett, with love and madness

ORCHARD BOOKS
96 Leonard Street, London EC2A 4XD
Orchard Books Australia
32/45-51 Huntley Street, Alexandria, NSW 2015
ISBN 1-84362-188-6
First published in Great Britain in 2004
A paperback original

A CIP catalogue record for this book is available from the British Library.
3 5 7 9 10 8 6 4 2
Printed in Great Britain

The Light Witch

Book 2: The Darkening

Andrew Matthews

ORCHARD BOOKS

Titles in *The Light Witch* Trilogy:

Shadowmaster

The Darkening

The Time of the Stars

Prologue: The Howling on the Hill

All the silver tabby cat's instincts told her that she was dying. For over a year she had lived wild, avoiding any contact with humans; now her health had broken and her strength was ebbing fast. Her neglected coat was grimy and matted, crusted matter clogged the corners of her eyes and her tattered ears bore the scars of many battles. Every few paces, the aching in her joints caused her to growl softly.

The cat felt no fear. She had heard the voice of death calling to her and she was moving through the night to meet it, under a sky bright with stars and the light of a three-quarter moon.

A car came along the road to the cat's right, the twin beams of its headlights gliding over hedgerows and farm gates. The cat froze, laid back her ears and hissed; then, after the car had passed without stopping, she carried on.

It took almost an hour to climb the hill. The silver tabby found the going hard and took frequent rests. When she came to a pool of fresh rainwater, she paused to drink. She could hear rats nearby, twittering in the darkness, but she had long lost interest in hunting or eating. Refreshed by the water, she continued her journey and reached the crest of the hill, and her goal.

The field had always been a quiet place, but tonight its silence was uncanny. The stones of the ancient circle at its centre stood stark and grim, silvered by the moon; some were tall, slender as blades; some rounded and squat. The cat crossed the field and entered the circle. She approached the tallest of the stones and sniffed at its base, then threw back her head and howled out a plea and a prayer.

The note in the cat's voice made the stone resonate. It glowed purple. Its surface liquified and rippled, slick and slow. A low throbbing sound pulsed through the air, like the beating of a huge heart.

The silver tabby pushed her head inside the liquid stone. It swallowed her shoulders and front legs, then her hind legs, and finally the tip of her tail.

The throbbing ceased; the purple glow faded away; silence returned to the circle.

Far below, at the foot of the hill, the street lights of a large town spread out in a twinkling orange net.

1
Witch Light

'Concentrate...concentrate...' Mum said.

Dido concentrated.

The air in front of her face thickened and turned glassy, distorting her view of the wall opposite. A bright fleck appeared and grew bigger, like the light on a train coming towards her through a tunnel. The fleck swelled into a globe the size of a tennis ball. The globe was a pale yellow, tinged with pink that swirled and feathered, reminding Dido of wet watercolour paints bleeding into one another. It gave off enough radiance to cast shadows that pitched and yawed as the globe swayed unsteadily.

'You're losing it!' said Mum. 'Hold it steady.'

Dido tried, but the globe had other ideas. It wobbled, then burst into miniature rockets and Catherine wheels before winking out.

Dido blinked away a swarm of ghostly after-images.

'I'll never get it right!' she groaned.

'You will,' said Mum. 'You're doing well – for a beginner. Witch lights are tricky at first. It's just a question of more practice.'

'And the point of all this would be?'

'Sorry?'

'What are witch lights for?'

'Er, to see in the dark?' Mum said.

Great! thought Dido. Now I feel dumb as well as a klutz.

'A witch light is a personal thing,' Mum continued. 'Each witch has her or his own and they're as individual as fingerprints. For Light Witches, like us, they're highly symbolic.'

'Do Shadowmasters have them?' said Dido.

Mum looked uneasy. Dido knew her mother didn't like it when she talked about Shadowmasters.

In ancient times, all magic had been the same, but at some point – Dido wasn't exactly sure when, why or how – it had split into Light Magic and Shadow Magic. Shadowmasters used Shadow Magic, which Light witches were forbidden to practise.

So it was just as well Mum didn't know that Dido *had* used Shadow Magic – and a lot of it – to defeat a Shadowmaster who'd tried to steal her magic. And if that wasn't bad enough for starters, the Shadowmaster had been one of the teachers at Dido's school. In destroying his magical power, Dido had caused him to lose his memory, and he'd had to take an early retirement. That had been over a year ago, when Dido was in Year Seven at the Prince Arthur Comprehensive School, where Mum was a Deputy Head.

'Try again,' said Mum.

Dido scowled.

'I've had it,' she said, 'and I've still got Maths homework to do.'

'Is that why you can't keep your mind on your magic?'

'Partly. Can we talk mother-to-daughter for a minute, instead of witch-to-witch?'

'All right,' said Mum.

'I'm worried about a friend of mine.'

'Is this one of those conversations that's supposed to be about a friend, but the friend is really you?' Mum asked.

'Huh? No, it's about a friend who's a friend. Actually, it's Philippa.'

'Philippa Trevelyan?'

'Do I have any other friends called Philippa?'

'Who knows?' said Mum. 'I can hardly keep track of you these days. Why are you worried about her?'

'You know her father remarried last summer? Philippa's having trouble with it.'

'In what way?'

'The usual. She resents her stepmother. It's like—'

'Dido,' Mum interrupted, 'please don't tell me any more. I'm Philippa's Deputy Head, remember? I shouldn't get involved in her affairs unless it affects her at school.'

'I don't want you to get involved, I want you to help me out.'

'How?'

'I thought you could teach me a spell that would—'

Mum shook her head. 'Absolutely not!' she said. 'Using magic to interfere with people's private lives is wrong.'

'I wouldn't be interfering. I'd just give Philippa a push in the right direction.'

'No, Dido. Philippa is far too young and impressionable, and so are you. If you used too much magic, or too little, you could make things far worse.'

Dido rolled her eyes in exasperation. It was the same old story: her parents held out on her about the really interesting spells because they were afraid of how she might use them, treating her as if she were a naughty little kid.

'How come you always assume that I'll mess up?' she said sullenly.

'I don't. It's just that…' Mum sighed. 'When I was your age I made some mistakes with magic and I hurt people without meaning to. I'm trying to save you from that.'

'What kind of mistakes?'

A year ago Mum wouldn't have said; now she seemed to have decided that Dido was old enough to know.

'There was a boy at my school – Simon Avery,' she said. 'I had an enormous crush on him, but he was sixteen, so he wasn't interested in a skinny thirteen-year-old girl. I cast a love charm on him.'

'You didn't!'

'I'm afraid I did,' Mum said, blushing.

'Did it work?'

'Too well. He followed me everywhere. I couldn't get rid of him. In the end, your gran phoned Simon's mother and threatened to ring the police if he didn't stop hanging around the house.'

'You turned an innocent boy into a stalker?' Dido teased. 'What happened after that?'

'I reversed the charm. Simon went from adoring me to loathing me. It wore off eventually, but for a fortnight he threw up whenever I passed him in the corridor. It must have been so embarrassing for him.'

Dido just about managed not to giggle.

'Did you ever use a love charm again?' she said.

'Never. I realised that it was cheating. It's better for people to like you for who you are, not because you make them. It's the same with Philippa. Let her find her own solutions to her problems.' Mum ran a hand through her hair. 'That's enough true-life confessions for one day. Go in and finish your homework. I'm going to stay here and meditate.'

Dido left the shed at the bottom of the back garden. The Nesbits called it the sanctuary as it contained herbs and potions, and the stone that was roughly shaped like a reclining goddess. Dido practised her magic there – or all the magic Mum and Dad knew about anyway.

As Dido walked into the house, she found her dad in the kitchen, rummaging in the part of the cupboard where the cat food was kept. Cosmo, an elderly black cat with amber eyes, weaved around him, making encouraging noises.

'Is it that time already?' Dido said.

'It's always that time as far as Cosmo's concerned,' said Dad. 'Listen to her nag.'

Dido listened.

'She's not nagging you, Dad,' she said. 'She's asking you not to give her tuna flakes. She had them yesterday.'

Dad looked over his shoulder at Cosmo and said, 'Is lamb with chicken OK?'

Cosmo purred that lamb with chicken would do nicely, thank you.

It was a joke among the Nesbits that Dido could understand what Cosmo was saying – at least, it was a joke with Mum and Dad, who didn't know that Dido actually *could* understand what Cosmo was saying. The cat wasn't only a pet, she was the family's familiar – a partner and guide in magic – and Dido's familiar in particular. They'd had some pretty spooky experiences together that Mum and Dad were unaware of, and Dido intended to keep it that way. If her parents found out what she and Cosmo had been up to, Dido would be grounded forever.

Dido spent the rest of Sunday afternoon slogging

away at Maths. Being a schoolgirl witch was nowhere near as appealing as it sounded. She had to work twice as hard as anyone else she knew to keep up with her lessons and her magic. Whenever she complained, Mum and Dad said the same thing, 'Being a Light Witch is a serious responsibility.'

There were times when Dido would gladly have traded in the responsibility for the kind of fun that normal nearly thirteen-year-olds had.

Philippa rang at seven. Dido's heart sank as soon as she heard the downbeat tone in Philippa's voice. Philippa had everything going for her: she was pretty, bright and had once been a good laugh; but ever since her father had remarried, all she did was moan.

'Hi, Philippa!' Dido said cheerfully, trying to gee things along. 'How you doing?'

'The same,' said Philippa. 'Guess where Alison went this morning?'

Alison was her stepmother.

'Where?' said Dido.

'To church! Can you believe that?'

'Um, it's Sunday, Philippa. Lots of people go to church.'

'Yeah, but she took my kid brother with her.

Tom's too young for all that supernatural stuff.'

Dido restrained herself from saying that if it wasn't for supernatural stuff, Philippa might still be under the spell that the Shadowmaster had used to make her float off the ground. They'd never talked about it in any detail, so Dido wasn't sure how much Philippa remembered about what had happened.

'What does your dad think?' said Dido.

'He says Tom should be allowed to make up his own mind.'

'Sounds fair to me.'

'How can it be fair? Dad goes along with everything Alison says, and Tom's just as bad. He *asked* to go to church with her.'

'Oh. So Alison didn't force him to?'

'Nothing so obvious. Alison twists people around her little finger. Like yesterday, in the supermarket...'

Dido settled into saying *yes* and *no* in the right places and let the rest wash over her.

When the conversation ended, Dido put down the phone, thought: I have to do something about this before Philippa bores me to death, and immediately felt ashamed for thinking it.

Hey, Dido! she told herself, that's no way to think about a friend.

Friendship was something new to Dido. Before the Nesbits had moved to Stanstowe, she hadn't had any friends because the fear of being found out as a witch had stopped her from getting close to anyone. She'd considered Philippa to be one of her best friends, but recently Philippa had seemed so irritating that Dido had begun to wonder.

Can friendship go off, like milk? she thought. Is that what's happening to Philippa and me?

She hoped not, and made up her mind to try and be more patient when Philippa had one of her moaning sessions.

2
Unwelcome Visitor

Next morning, the weather was so bright that when Dido left the house to catch the bus to school, she noticed for the first time that spring had arrived. Daffodils and crocuses were out in the neighbourhood gardens, and blossoming cherry trees looked like bridesmaids. It made Dido think of new beginnings, and of her own new beginning in particular.

In a few weeks she'd be thirteen – a teenager. More importantly, a Light Witch's thirteenth birthday was a significant event, marking the boundary between childhood and adulthood. The tradition went back hundreds of years – if not thousands. In ancient times, witches had gathered in groups of thirteen, known as covens, and in honour of the ancient custom, when a Light Witch reached the age of thirteen, it was called a Covening. Not that Dido was expecting thirteen people at her Covening. It would be a low-key celebration – just her, Mum, Dad and Cosmo. Even so, she could hardly wait. Apart from the buzz of being able to think of herself as a teenager rather than a kid, she hoped that after her Covening, Mum and Dad would let her in on some of the magical secrets they'd been unwilling to reveal so far. There was a lot to look forward to.

As Dido approached the bus stop, she saw other Prince Arthur pupils waiting ahead of her. The only one who didn't seem to be suffering from a bad attack of Monday morning was Scott Pink, who enjoyed going to school for the peace and quiet. Scott's parents were divorced. He had a brother at university, a sister in Year Ten, and with a younger brother and sister as well, life at home was pretty hectic. His mother worked from Monday to Saturday, and Scott helped out with cooking, cleaning and sorting out family quarrels.

Dido and Scott had met at the bus stop on their very first day at the comp. Scott had been a bit of a runt back then, but he'd sprouted until he was as tall as Dido, and developed to-die-for, long eyelashes. Dido suspected that he might have the makings of a hunk, but she didn't tell Scott because it would've been pointless. Scott's main interest wasn't girls, but escapology and stage magic. Dido had told him right off that she was a witch. He didn't believe her at first, but when it had finally sunk in that Dido had been telling the truth, Scott had accepted it without a fuss, and the friendship had cemented.

'Morning, Dido!' Scott said with a broad grin. 'Good weekend?'

'So so,' said Dido. 'I had to practise making a witch light, so I can see in the dark.'

Scott frowned.

'Wouldn't it be easier to buy a torch?' he said. 'I had a great weekend. I invented a new trick.'

'Oh?' Dido said cautiously, remembering the other tricks that Scott had invented. 'Does it involve ropes and handcuffs?'

'Nope. Just ordinary playing cards.' Scott produced a pack from his school bag. 'Check 'em out.'

Dido sifted through the pack.

'You're right, they're ordinary,' she said.

'Exactly! They haven't been marked or interfered with in any way. Now, choose any card you like, memorise it and put it face down on top of the pack.'

Dido followed Scott's instructions.

'Tell me what it was,' said Scott.

'The Three of Clubs.'

Scott reached out and turned over the top card; it was the Three of Clubs.

'Cor-rect!' he said. 'Great trick, huh?'

Dido laughed in spite of herself.

'I wonder about you at times,' she said.

'That's because I'm wonderful. Any news of Philippa?'

'Yeah. She rang me on Friday night. And Saturday, and last night.'

'And?'

'She's so depressed, it's making *me* depressed. I'm not sure how much more I can take. If she doesn't cheer up soon, we're going to have a bust-up.'

Scott drew nearer and lowered his voice. 'Couldn't you, er...?' He waggled his fingers like a cartoon wizard casting a spell.

'My mum won't teach me how.'

Scott thought for a moment, then said, 'What Philippa needs is something to take her out of herself.'

'Such as?'

'A hobby? A boyfriend?' said Scott. 'Hey, maybe she could combine the two and knit herself a boyfriend!'

*

At school, Philippa was outside C block, like most of the rest of Eight North, only she stood a little way off from the others, as if she wanted people to notice that she wasn't being noticed. As Dido and Scott drew near, Philippa suddenly turned and hurried off in the opposite direction.

She's trying to emotionally blackmail us! Dido thought, and a fierce surge of anger took her by surprise. She knew that she was overreacting, but the anger seemed to have a mind of its own and kept growing and growing.

Dido pictured a flat blue sea and a thread of Golden Syrup spinning off a spoon, and used the images to cast a calming spell on herself.

'What's with Philippa?' Scott said.

'She's playing power games,' said Dido. 'We're supposed to go after her and ask what's the matter.'

'But we're not?'

'I don't think it would be a good idea to give in to her,' Dido said.

Scott was uneasy. Dido and Philippa were two of the three friends he'd made at school. If they fell out he'd be stuck in the middle, and if he chose sides he'd lose most of his audience.

'Are you sure we shouldn't?' he said.

'Definitely,' said Dido. 'It'll be better if we wait until she comes to us.'

Dido didn't tell Scott the real reason why it would be better to wait, which was that she was afraid she might lose her temper again and have a massive row with Philippa.

What's wrong with me? Dido thought. Why am I letting Philippa get to me like this?

It was puzzling and worrying.

Philippa didn't come near Dido and Scott all morning. Dido had made up her mind not to give in and make the first move, but at lunchtime she cracked and went to sit with Philippa in the cafeteria. Scott joined them. Dido was waiting for the right moment to say something tactful, but Scott blundered in with both feet.

'Why the long face, Philippa?' he said. 'Forget to take your happy pills this morning?'

Philippa shot Scott a look that would have brought a species to the brink of extinction.

'It's my stepmother,' she said.

'Is she being too strict with you?'

'No. She smarms around me. She wants

us to be friends.'

Scott frowned.

'What's wrong with that?' he said.

Philippa snorted. 'She doesn't mean it. She wants to take over and play happy families.'

'And you don't want to live in a happy family?' said Scott, using his fork to harpoon a chip.

'We *were* happy, until she moved in.'

Scott placed a reassuring hand on Philippa's shoulder and said, 'Things'll sort themselves out. Just give it time.'

Which was exactly the wrong thing to say.

Philippa stood up, bumping the table; her fork fell on to the floor.

'You don't understand, do you?' she said. 'No one understands!'

Scott watched open-mouthed as Philippa stormed out of the cafeteria.

'What did I do?' he asked Dido.

'Not a lot,' Dido said. 'She takes everything the wrong way at the moment.'

'What's her problem?'

'She thinks she wants her stepmother out of the way, but that isn't it.'

'Isn't it?'

'No,' said Dido. 'Philippa's problem is that she wants her mother to be alive.'

Philippa walked blindly across the campus, past the tennis courts and the car park, and round to the back of the Sports Hall, where a small group of Year Ten boys puffed furtively on cigarettes. She didn't stop until she came to the wire fence at the edge of the playing fields.

Her feelings were a mess. She was confused, and angry in a way that made her turn her anger against herself. None of her power games had worked, and she was worried that she might be losing her friends.

'Who needs friends anyway?' she muttered sullenly. 'I can manage OK on my own!'

And then, suddenly, Philippa found that she wasn't on her own.

A silver tabby cat padded towards her, mewing plaintively. It was an unusual-looking animal: its yellow eyes were a fraction too close together, its ears were ragged and when the sunlight caught the dark markings on its coat, they shone purple.

'Hi, Moggy,' Philippa said. 'Are your mates giving you a hard time too?'

The cat stood at Philippa's feet and pranced;

she reached down to stroke its head.

Without warning, the silver tabby hissed, and lashed out with a front paw. Philippa felt its claws rake the back of her hand.

'Ow!' she cried.

She glanced at the white scratches on her skin. Dark beads of blood welled up, and she raised her hand to her mouth to lick them away.

'Spiteful thing!' she said. 'Why did you—'

The cat had gone. Philippa looked from left to right along the entire length of the fence, but she couldn't see the silver tabby anywhere.

As they were heading for home at the end of school, Scott elbowed Dido in the ribs. 'Miss Morgan looks like she's having a bad-hair day, doesn't she?'

Dido followed the direction of Scott's gaze.

Miss Morgan was in the staff car park. She was standing beside her car, ignition keys held at the ready, but she was frozen, as though she'd forgotten what she was doing.

Miss Morgan taught Drama. She was young, pretty and popular, but she had a secret that few people knew about: in fact, she didn't even know about it herself.

Dido had once suspected that Miss Morgan was a

witch, and she'd managed to be right and wrong at the same time. It was Mum who had straightened Dido out. According to Mum, Miss Morgan was a Sleeper, someone who had magical powers without being aware of them.

Dido thought it must be awful. Magic came from inside, and if it was untrained, could cause all kinds of mischief.

I'd go crazy if I didn't know about my magic, thought Dido. I'd be afraid that I was cracking up.

'Dido?' said Scott.

'Huh?'

'Why have you stopped walking?'

'I haven't,' said Dido, taking a step forwards.

'You're scratching your thumbs.'

'Am I?'

'Do they itch?'

'Would I be scratching them if they didn't?'

Scott screwed up his eyes.

'Your thumbs always itch before something weird happens, don't they?' he said.

'Not always,' said Dido. 'They didn't itch before I met you, and you're weird.'

But though she'd attempted to turn it into a joke, Dido knew that Scott was right.

*

In the middle of the night, Cosmo tried to wake Dido by dabbing at Dido's bottom lip with a velveted paw. When that failed to work, Cosmo extended her claws and tried again.

'What the— Cut it out, Cosmo!' Dido spluttered. 'I'll feed you in the morning.'

Cosmo walked over Dido's chest, chattering rapidly.

'Whoa!' said Dido. 'Slow down, will you? There's a *what* in the garden?'

Cosmo used a term that Dido didn't understand.

'Say that last part again?'

Cosmo said something quite different, and she didn't mean it as a compliment.

'OK, OK,' said Dido. 'Don't get a blonk on.'

She hauled herself out of bed, went to the window and drew back the curtain.

It was a clear night. Stars glittered in the sky above the roofs of the houses across the way.

'So,' said Dido. 'I'm looking at the garden. It has plants in it – big deal! You interrupted my beauty sleep to show me this? I—'

At the bottom of the garden, something moved. A light floated around the side of the sanctuary and hovered at the door. The light was green, streaked with orange, changing to turquoise and blue, then shades of grey. It went up and down and from side to side.

It's a witch light and it's looking for a way into the sanctuary, Dido thought.

The witch light went out, almost as if Dido's thought had extinguished it.

Dido turned to Cosmo.

'I don't know about you, but I think we might have an unwanted visitor on our hands,' she said.

3
Lifting the Veil

When Philippa got home after school, she found that the lounge had been turned into a tip. The floor was strewn with empty cardboard boxes, plastic bags and a pile of polystyrene packaging that looked like a collapsed igloo. Dad was on his knees in the middle of it all, muttering under his breath as he tried to connect a cable to a grey cube. He looked up when Philippa entered the room and smiled sheepishly, as if he'd been caught raiding the fridge in the night.

'What are you doing?' Philippa asked.

'I was hoping to have it set up by the time you came home,' said Dad. 'I've been following the instructions, but they don't seem to have taken me anywhere I wanted to go.'

'Instructions for what?'

Dad waved at the chaos around him.

'This lot,' he said. 'Computer, monitor, printer. My

company's finally decided to enter the twenty-first century. Once I've got the computer going, I can get on-line and do more work from home. It saves on travelling expenses and time. Do you know how many hours I waste commuting to the office in an average week?'

Philippa didn't know and didn't particularly want to, but Dad told her anyway. He also threw in a lot of stuff about fossil fuels, exhaust fumes and the environment; he made it sound like having a computer was going to help him to save the world.

'And you and Tom can use it to do homework,' he added.

'Oh, super!' Philippa said sarcastically.

'You can play games, e-mail your friends—'

'I don't need to e-mail my friends. I talk to them.'

'I know. I get to pay the phone bill.'

'I don't ring my friends that much!' Philippa protested. 'Tom's the one. When he rang Mike last night, he was on the phone for over—'

Dad held up his hand.

'It's not a blame game,' he said. 'I was only joking. Fancy giving me a hand?'

'I don't know that much about computers,' Philippa said with a shrug.

'Don't you use them at school?'

'Yes, but the teachers assemble them. I wouldn't know where to start.'

'Me neither. Shame, I was hoping you could tell me what a printer port is.'

Philippa glanced over Dad's shoulder at the framed photograph of Alison. The frame had once held a picture of Mum. Philippa wondered if Dad had thrown Mum's photo away, or placed Alison's photo on top of it. Then she noticed how quiet the house was: no TV blaring, no CD player shaking the walls, no bleeping Game Boy.

'Where's Tom?' she said.

'Alison's taken him shopping.'

'What for?'

'Clothes, I think. I wanted him out of the way so the computer would be a surprise.'

Alison, of course, would have leapt at the chance to get Tom alone. Philippa could just imagine them in a clothes shop, Tom posing and goofing around, Alison laughing, pretending that he was funny. How could Tom do that, how could he betray Mum that way?

'I'm going up to my room,' said Philippa.

Dad made his eyes big and round.

'Sure you can't spare the time to help your poor old father?' he said in his You-are-Daddy's-best-girl voice.

'Too much homework.'

Philippa was lying, but if she stayed, it would be like she approved of what Dad was doing, and she didn't approve of anything that Dad did any more.

The computer was still in pieces when Alison and Tom returned from town. Tom gave a whoop when he saw the hardware and put it together in two minutes, explaining to Dad as he went along.

'See, the thing goes into the thing, and the other thing plugs in that thing.'

Alison left them to it, went into the kitchen and found Philippa sipping a glass of orange juice.

Alison smiled, but her eyes were cautious.

'Boys and their toys, eh?' she said.

Philippa didn't respond.

'What's wrong with your hand?' said Alison.

'Nothing,' Philippa said, putting her left hand behind her back where Alison couldn't see it. 'It's just a scratch.'

'It looks sore. You ought to let me put some antiseptic cream on it.'

Philippa glowered.

'I can put on my own antiseptic cream, thanks,' she said. 'I'm not a baby.'

She left the kitchen, went up to the bathroom and looked at her hand more closely. Alison was right, the scratches *did* look sore.

'I hope that mangy stray hasn't infected me with something,' Philippa thought.

It was another item to add to her catalogue of woes.

After dinner, Tom showed Dad and Philippa how to surf the Net, while Alison sat on the sofa, reading a newspaper.

'Shall we look at the Stanstowe website?' said Tom.

'Why bother?' said Philippa. 'We live there.'

Tom rattled away on the keyboard, and a page appeared on the monitor.

Just above Stanstowe, Philippa saw:

STANSHAWE, JAMES LAYTON (1914 - 1988),
BIOGRAPHICAL DETAILS

'What's that?' she said, pointing at the screen.

'You get loads of stuff like that,' Tom told her. 'After someone dies, the family builds a site for them, a memorial thing so they can live forever on the Web. Kind of spooky, isn't it?'

'We ought to do one for Mum,' Philippa said.

The room seemed to grow colder.

Dad wriggled in his chair, cleared his throat and said, 'We don't have to. We can remember her without a website, and you and Tom are her memorial.'

Bet Alison wishes we weren't, Philippa thought. She's got Dad, now she's after everything that used to be Mum's.

She glanced at Alison. Alison's face was hidden by the newspaper, but Philippa could tell by the way she was sitting that Alison felt uncomfortable. Dad went over to the sofa, sat beside Alison and began talking quietly.

'Why d'you do that?' Tom muttered.

'What?'

'Talk about Mum all the time.'

'Because no one else does.'

Tom was hurting, close to tears. 'Mum's dead, Philippa!' he said.

Philippa tapped herself on the chest. 'Not in here, she isn't.'

She hoped that she'd said it loudly enough for Dad and Alison to hear.

*

Later on, in bed, Philippa wondered about the frozen place inside her that wouldn't defrost. She knew she was being deliberately awkward and stroppy around Alison, but she couldn't stop it. Alison wanted to replace Mum, and Philippa wasn't about to let her.

'I'm not giving in, Mum!' she whispered to the ceiling. 'I'm never going to forget you!'

Philippa fell asleep stroking the scratches on the back of her hand, and almost at once fell into a disturbingly vivid dream. She was in a dark chamber, lit by a burning torch fixed to a wall. The light from the torch wavered over roughly hewn stone blocks that glistened with moisture, and the air smelled of damp earth.

There was a rustling sound behind her. Philippa turned and saw her mother, dressed in a long grey shift with a frayed hem. Her dark hair was loose, straggling across her face.

'Mum!' Philippa said joyfully. 'I thought you were dead.'

'I am,' said Mum, 'but I can live in your dreams.'

Her voice was huskier than Philippa remembered, and as dry as cobwebs.

'Whenever you dream, I will be there keeping

watch over you,' Mum said.

Philippa felt odd. The figure in front of her was unmistakably her mother, but also seemed to be someone else.

'Is it really you?' Philippa said.

'How can you doubt it, Pip?'

Warmth washed over Philippa. 'Pip!' she said. 'I haven't let anyone call me that since you—' She couldn't bring herself to finish the sentence.

'Death is merely a veil between those who live in the world and those who live outside it,' said Mum. 'You may lift that veil whenever you choose.'

More oddness: Mum's speech was stiff and formal, as if she were speaking on the phone to a stranger. Her eyes, once grey, had turned violet.

'Listen to me, Pip,' Mum said. 'You must learn how to use the new machine.'

'You mean the computer – why?'

'Do as I say!' Mum said sharply. 'I am your mother. You will obey me without question.'

'Yes, Mum. Without question.'

Even though it was only a dream, Philippa didn't want her mother to get upset.

★ ★ ★ ★ ★ ★ ★

4
The World Machine

The school bus dropped her at the corner of the street at the regular time. As she got off, Doogie the driver said what he always said, 'See ya tomorrow, Princess.'

And she said what she always said back, 'Yeah, see ya – wouldn't wanna be ya!'

Doogie laughed, closed the doors of the bus and drove off into the heavy downtown traffic.

Same old, same old.

All the houses in the street had flights of steps going up to their front doors. Everybody called the steps 'stoops', which was an old Dutch word or something. Below the steps were concrete wells and basement windows. People grew all kinds of plants and stuff in tubs in the wells, and also in window boxes. You had your ferns, your palms, and the bright flowers she loved so much that she'd found out their name and memorised it. They were zinnias – way cool! When she was older, she was going to tell all her friends to call her Zinnia, or Zinny maybe – yeah, Zinny sounded better.

Above the roofs of the houses stood the distant tops of the tall buildings that were part of one of the world's most famous skylines. She didn't pay them any attention though – they'd always been there; this was home.

Halfway down the street she passed an asphalt playground. Kids were out, horsing around as they played basketball; elderly people watched them from wooden benches, envying their energy.

A heavily accented male voice shouted, 'Hey, Francis! Over here, over here!'

He must have missed the shot, because just after came the sound of loud laughter.

It made her smile; she got a big kick out of other people's happiness.

Climbing the stoop to her own front door, she paused to wave to Mrs Aaronson, knowing she'd be sitting at the window of her first-floor apartment across the way. Mrs Aaronson didn't go out much; she stayed by her window all day, watching people passing by in the street. She liked being waved to.

The hallway was dark and quiet after the noise and sunshine outside. She closed the front door, shrugged off her backpack and hung up her jacket on *the row of pegs near the wall-mounted phone.*

'Hey, Mom! I'm home!'

Mom was sure to be in the kitchen, baking something; boy, was she ever crazy about baking. What would it be today, bread or cupcakes?

She took a long slow breath in through her nose, and frowned. Instead of the rich yeasty smell she'd expected, the air was dank. Puzzled, she walked down the hall and stopped in the kitchen doorway.

Mom wasn't in the kitchen; it looked like nobody had been there for years. All the work surfaces and cupboards were coated in a grey fur of dust. Something had boiled over on the cooker, leaving a brown stain on the enamel.

Mom was too picky to ever let that happen. Mom would have wiped up the mess right away, and then cleaned the entire kitchen until it sparkled. Dad had cracked a joke about it one time, when the dishwasher was acting up: 'Let's eat dinner off of the floor tonight – it's cleaner than the plates!'

And then she remembered that she was dead.

She fought hard against the memory, struggling to keep a hold on the house and the street and the city, but they slipped away. The shadows in the kitchen seeped into the walls and spread like black ink soaking into a piece of blotting paper.

The kitchen went away; darkness stretched out in all directions, forever.

She wrapped her arms around herself and shivered.

'No!' she whimpered. 'It's real! My house is there. My mom and dad are there!'

'You are wrong, child,' said a voice. 'They are illusions, drawn from your recollections of the past. Only the darkness is real.'

The voice was masculine, deep and rich as molasses; she turned in the direction it had come from.

'Where are you?' she said.

'Close by. Give me your hand.'

She reached out her arm and felt something shaped like a hand envelop her own.

'What is this place?' she said. 'I've been here before, and it sucks!'

'It has many names,' said the voice. 'None of them matters. I sense that you are not yet ready.'

'Ready for what?'

'To leave behind what came before this.'

She thought about what had been before – Mom and Dad, her friends at school, her whole life – and said, 'I guess not. Does that make me a bad person?'

'Merely a lost traveller,' said the voice. Its hand tugged gently at her. 'Come with me. I wish to

show you something.'

She let herself be led over to her left – and there was a light. In all the time she'd spent in the darkness, it was the only light she'd seen that she hadn't made herself. What was that wacky colour called – violet, magenta, lilac?

'Look deeper,' said the voice. 'Tell me what you see.'

She saw more light, in streams that intersected and made patterns; blizzards of numbers travelling along straight lines that were like microchip circuits, or streets. She heard beeps, buzzes and voices, millions of voices, gabbling at high speed.

'Is that a city or the inside of a machine?' she said.

'Both and more,' said the voice. 'It is a world, and it can be your world, a refuge from the dark.'

'How do I get there?'

'It lies within my power to open a portal, if it is your desire to enter.'

'Are you kidding? You bet I want to enter!' she said enthusiastically. Then, fearing that she might have caused offence by sounding too greedy, she added, 'Will you be in there with me?'

'I am everywhere,' said the voice.

She didn't know whether the World Machine expanded or she shrank, but suddenly she was inside. She looked around, jaw dropping as she took in the neon skyscrapers *and wide boulevards. Cars and taxis moved so quickly that her eyes couldn't follow them.*

The voice was at her side. It had a form now: a man in a beige trench coat and a big soft hat, the brim snapped down to cover his eyes.

'Where do I start?' she gasped.

The man smiled; under the shadow of his hat, he glowed with a purple phosphorescence.

'At the beginning,' he said. 'I will take you there. It is not far.'

5
Storme

Tuesday morning was mayhem in the Nesbit house. Mum's alarm clock hadn't gone off and she was running late – almost literally running. She zipped from room to room, gathering files together, a half-eaten piece of toast wedged in her mouth. When Dido came downstairs, Mum nearly collided with her as she rushed for the front door.

'Mum,' Dido said, 'there was a—'

'Can't stop!' said Mum, spraying crumbs. 'Tell me tonight.'

Dido went into the kitchen. Dad was at the oven, stirring the contents of a saucepan. He wasn't in a hurry because he worked at home, writing articles and reviews for computer magazines.

'Scrambled eggs?' he said.

'Yes please,' said Dido.

Dad heaped the contents on to a plate.

'That's way too much!' said Dido.

'Your mother didn't have time for hers. I hate wasting food.'

Cosmo, who was sitting on the work surface with her tail wrapped around her paws, made a suggestion.

'Greedy-guts!' said Dido.

'Who, me?' said Dad.

'No. Cosmo. She says she'll eat Mum's share.'

'Dream on!' Dad said to Cosmo.

Dad carried the plates of scrambled eggs into the dining room.

Dido sat opposite him and said, 'Dad?'

Dad's mind was elsewhere.

'Alarm clock,' he murmured, thinking out loud.

'Huh?'

'I must remember to buy a new alarm clock today.'

'What's the matter with the old one?'

'Your mother lost her temper and melted it.'

Dido was impressed.

'Cool!' she said. 'Which spell did she use?'

'Not one I'm going to tell you about. Eat your eggs.'

Dido decided not to pester Dad. It wasn't long until her Covening, and he'd have to tell her any spell she wanted to know after that. She waited a few minutes, then said, 'Did you or Mum make any magic last night?'

'No, why?'

'I saw a witch light in the back garden.'

Dad's forkful of eggs paused halfway to his mouth.

'Are you sure?' he said.

'I know a witch light when I see one, Dad. It was outside the sanctuary and it acted like it wanted in.'

'What time was this?'

'Midnight.'

Dad frowned.

'Why didn't you fetch me or your mother?' he said.

'Because it disappeared.'

'What colour was it?'

'All kinds of colours. It kept changing.'

Dad's frown deepened.

'Funny thing though,' said Dido. 'It couldn't have been lighting anyone's way, because there was nobody there.'

'Witch lights do more than light the way,' Dad said thoughtfully. 'Skilled witches can send them to look at things long distance.'

'Like spying?'

'Sort of.'

'Who'd want to spy on our sanctuary?' said Dido.

'Can't have been anyone who meant us any harm. Witch lights are a Light Witch thing, aren't they?'

'Not necessarily.'

Aha! thought Dido. So Shadowmasters have witch lights too. Interesting!

Philippa was half dozing, exploring a daydream that branched out in different directions, but each branch ended the same way – no Alison. She imagined Dad and Alison having a massive row; Dad kicking Alison out because he'd finally twigged what sort of person she was; Alison leaving Dad because she'd found a better victim to feed on. Philippa's favourite part of the daydream was when Dad said, 'I should have listened to you, Philippa. You were right about Alison all along.'

The beeping of the alarm clock broke the dream. Philippa groaned, switched off the alarm and tried to return to her imagination, but it was no good. Maybe she could fall asleep, like Sleeping Beauty, and not wake up until she was sixteen, old enough to leave home.

Downstairs was the usual morning chaos. Alison seemed to be everywhere, straightening Dad's tie, fussing over Tom, diving in and out of the kitchen, controlling everything. 'Good morning, Philippa,' she said. 'Sleep well?'

'Mmm,' said Philippa.

'What can I get you for breakfast?'

'I'll get it myself.'

'It's no trouble. What would you like?'

'Er, to be left alone?'

Philippa slouched into the dining room, sat down, poured cereal flakes and milk into a bowl and began to eat. The crunch of the flakes drowned the hissing sound leaking out of the headphones of Tom's personal stereo.

'Want to come shopping with me this afternoon?' Dad said. 'I can pick you up from school.'

'What are we buying?'

'A digital camera. You can help me to choose which one.'

'Who else is going?'

'Just you and me.'

Dad's smile appeared just a little too wide.

Oh, I get it! Philippa thought. He wants me on my own so we can have a deep-and-meaningful about Alison.

'You'd be better off taking Tom with you,' she said.

'Could be fun.'

'What, standing around in a shop while you and the assistant bang on about a load of stuff I don't understand? I don't think so.'

Dad looked disappointed and there was a gleam of annoyance in his eyes, but he let it drop.

'Suit yourself,' he said.

'I'm going to.'

Why did he let her get away with talking to him like that? If he was angry, why didn't he give her a telling-off?

Because he's scared, Philippa thought. He's scared that I'll shout back and tell him the truth, and he won't be able to handle it.

Dad leaned over, prised the headphones off Tom's ears and said, 'How about you?'

'How about me what?' said Tom.

'Want to help me pick a digital camera after school?'

'I've already picked one – a CNZ 3800. We could go and buy it, though.'

'Is it good?'

'No idea, but it looks the business.'

Dad cocked an eyebrow at Philippa; she looked down into her cereal bowl.

*

On her way to school, Philippa found Ollie hanging around the postbox at the end of her street. Ollie – real name Oliver Falkener – had become friends with Philippa and Dido when they were in Year Seven, but though he went to the same school, he was in a different form: Eight West. Ollie was quite good-looking, with his dark red hair and bright green eyes, but he wasn't Philippa's type. This was a shame in some ways, because Ollie was a lot more sympathetic and considerate than Dido or Scott. He always made time to listen to Philippa's troubles, and didn't seem to mind how long it took.

'Waiting for someone, Ollie?' Philippa said.

'You, of course – who else?'

They crossed over Hazelwood Close into Chestnut Road.

'How are you?' asked Ollie.

'How d'you think?'

Ollie narrowed his eyes and made a pantomime of rubbing his chin.

'Hmm! I'd say that you were having an orange day today,' he said.

'Excuse me?'

'Don't you ever get that thing where you get a colour that tells you what mood people are in?' said

Ollie. 'Like if they're happy, they'll be something bright, like a sunshine yellow, and if they're miserable, they're a darker colour.'

'Er, no!' said Philippa, sounding as if she didn't have a clue what Ollie was talking about.

'Oh,' said Ollie. 'I guess it must just be me then.'

Actually, Ollie didn't need to guess – he knew that it was just him. His grandmother had been a Light Witch, and though he hadn't inherited all her magical powers, he had second sight, an ability to sense what others couldn't sense. He was sensitive to people's auras, the energy field that they radiated, and sometimes he had dreams that foretold the future. It was one of the reasons he was mates with Dido. He'd recognised that she was a witch the first moment they'd met, and she'd talked to him about things she couldn't discuss with anyone else.

'What does orange mean?' said Philippa.

'That you're in the mood for getting stuff sorted.'

Ollie was lying. Philippa's orange aura indicated that she was disturbed to the point of turmoil. It was the strongest aura he'd seen around Philippa, so strong that he wondered if she might be hiding something with it. Ollie could almost make out another colour behind the orange. If he could only—

'It isn't me who ought to get stuff sorted, it's my dad,' Philippa said. Her aura changed to an impenetrable dark grey.

Philippa spent the day avoiding her friends. At the end of school she hid in the loos until everything went quiet, in case they were waiting for her. When she came out, the silence made her shudder. The school felt creepy, empty but not empty, as if all the pupils and teachers who had ever been there had returned as ghosts. She seemed to hear an eerie voice whispering.

Then, as she turned a corner, Philippa got a shock. Miss Morgan was standing in the middle of the corridor, muttering to herself. Her arms were stretched up, her eyes were closed and her long hair was whipping around her head, as if a wind were blowing through it.

Only there was no wind.

'Miss Morgan?' said Philippa.

Miss Morgan opened her eyes and lowered her hands. Her hair fell back into place.

'Are you all right, Miss?'

'Yes,' said Miss Morgan speaking quickly. 'I'm sorry

if I startled you. I didn't know anyone was still here. The Stanstowe Amateur Dramatic Society is holding auditions tonight for a production. I was just practising my piece.'

'I'm sure you'll get a part, Miss.'

'And what are you doing here this late?'

'Nothing, Miss. I'm on my way home,' Philippa said.

The house was blissfully Alison-free, and Dad and Tom were still in town. Philippa chugged down a can of cola and let out a loud burp.

I'd better make the most of the time to myself, she thought. What'll I do – start my homework? Not really. TV?

Then she remembered the computer, and the promise she'd made to Mum in her dream.

Philippa went into the lounge, turned on the computer and gave it a good checking out. She played Patience for a while, then decided to find out what e-mail was all about. It was simple to set up an account: she just clicked on the right files, and little boxes came up, giving her instructions.

Enter e-mail address.

Philippa typed, *philippa trevelyan*, then deleted it.

That wasn't who she was, it was too boring. She typed, *storme.* It was the first name of some actress she'd once seen in a made-for-TV movie. The actress had been lousy and so had the movie, but the name had stuck in Philippa's mind. It looked great: *storme@bpm.net.*

Philippa pressed **ENTER**.

So far so good, but now what? Philippa knew lots of people who were on the net, but not their e-mail addresses. She wanted to contact somebody. Was there an e-mail directory where she could look up names?

While Philippa was puzzling, the computer suddenly made a tinkling noise, and a box popped on to the screen labelled 'Chatline' at the top. Inside the box was:

H-e-e-y, Storme!!! How ya doin?

Philippa said, 'Huh?'

6
Chat

Philippa gazed in astonishment at the screen.

A second message came up.

What gives, Storme? Cat got your tongue?

Philippa clicked on the RESPOND button and typed: Who are you?

Can't you read? I'm Zinny!! Oh, wait a second, you must be able to read, because you can write. LOL!

LOL?

It means Laugh Out Loud. I thought everybody knew that. Where have you been hiding yourself?

Nowhere. I've never been on-line before.

Welcome to Cyberspace!! You'll love it. It's neat.

How did you find out my e-mail address? I only set it up just now.

Something pulled me to it. I know my way around, Storme. I've been places you would NOT believe.

There's a lot of weird dudes out there on the Net - and I know because I'm one!!!

LOL.

Thank you kindly. So are you a boy or a girl, Storme? How old are you?

Girl. Thirteen.

Hey, me too. Small world, huh? What are you like?

This was such an unexpectedly difficult question that it took Philippa several seconds to think of an answer.

I don't know. Ordinary, I suppose.

Ordinary??!! You're on a chatline and you're telling people you're ORDINARY? You can say you're anything you want. You can say you're a mega-babe mantrap, like me. ROFL!!

Roll On Floor Laughing?

You catch on quick.

What are you like?

Flaky. Wacky. L-O-U-D!! My mom says that I talk too much, but I tell her it's because I've got a lot to say. I have like this totally depressing straight mousy hair and I have to wear an orthodontal brace. You ever had one?

No.

Don't!! You never get to make out. There was this girl I knew who wore a brace? She went on a date to the

movies with this guy who had braces also. They started necking and their braces locked. They had to have emergency surgery to get separated.

Are you serious?

Never - I don't have the time.

You're American, aren't you?

You betcha!!! I don't live in the States any more though.

Where do you live?

There was a long pause.

Zinny, are you still there?

Uh-huh.

You didn't answer my question.

It's kind of complicated. I move around a lot.

Where are you now?

Chatting to you. You're a Brit, right?

Right.

You live in London?

Stanstowe. It's about 80 kilometres from London.

Is it like one of those Olde Worlde places with thatched cottages and roses round the door?

No. It's pretty boring. Most of the houses look the same. So do the people who live in them.

LOL!! And what about you, Storme? What are you REALLY like?

Right now? I think depressed is the word.

Boyfriend trouble?

Family trouble.

Tell me about it. Families suck, don't they? Is your mom giving you a hard time?

She died three years ago.

Ouch! Guess that must be tough.

It is. What makes it tougher is that now I have a stepmother, Alison.

You no like?

She comes on like she's my real mother, when she's not.

Does she try too hard?

Yes. Why am I telling you this?

Because you don't know me. Sometimes it's easier to talk to a stranger. That's what happens on chatlines. People come out with like TOTALLY personal stuff.

Is that what you do?

All depends on whether I like who I'm talking to. Should that be - whom I'm talking to?

Pass.

Say what?

It means I don't know. How can you tell you like someone if you haven't met them?

Because writing to them is easy. You forget about the keyboard, so it feels like you're actually talking. What

are the guys like in Stanstowe? Any eye candy?

I suppose.

You dating anyone?

No. My father says I'm a bit young for that sort of thing.

Wise up, sis!! There is NO SUCH THING as too young!! Anyone ever asked you out on a date?

Once. A boy called Greg.

And?

Nothing. I said no. He had a weight problem.

FATTIST!!

And he picked his nose.

Eew, gross!

Does that make me a noseist?

Who cares? Uh-oh! Look, this has been a lot of fun, Storme, but I have to go now. Catch you again some time?

I'd like that. Can I have your e-mail address?

Why?

So I can e-mail you.

DOH!! No can do, sorry. I'm not supposed to be on-line in the first place. If you sent me an e-mail I'd be in B-I-G trouble!

How can I contact you?

You can't. I'll contact you. Bye!

The chatline box vanished.

Philippa felt pleased. She'd followed the advice her mother had given her in the dream, and now she had a new friend. It was the best thing that had happened to her for ages.

Dad, Alison and Tom had obviously been shopping together and had a great time, because they were laughing when they came in. Dad held up a plastic carrier bag that was emblazoned with the logos of Japanese electronics companies.

'Ta-da!' he said. 'We are officially digital.'

'Good for us,' said Philippa.

Tom was hyper. He snatched the bag from Dad, emptied it, wrestled the camera out of its packaging and started babbling about pixels, red eye mode and image-manipulation software.

Philippa said, 'I'm sorry, Tom. Is all that supposed to mean something?'

'And there's no waiting!' Tom raved. 'There's a monitor on the back so you can see the picture straightaway.' Tom pressed a button; the camera flashed. 'Look!' He held the camera out to Philippa.

'Wow!' Philippa said. 'A picture of the lounge. Amazing.'

'Yeah, but you can download the picture on to the computer and fiddle about with it,' said Tom. 'You can make it lighter, darker, change the colours so the walls are bright orange – anything you like.'

'Sounds neat.'

Tom wrinkled one side of his nose.

'Neat?' he said. 'Only American say neat.'

Philippa smiled, then noticed that Alison and Dad were staring at her, and said, 'What?'

'You're smiling,' said Dad. 'I'd forgotten how much it suits you.'

'Well excuse me! I'll try to remember that I'm supposed to be miserable all the time, OK?'

Dad sighed and glanced at Alison, who shrugged.

Philippa knew that they'd been discussing her, and wondered what they'd said.

7
Lord of the Night

Scott was unhappy. All day Philippa had kept her distance; she didn't sit with him and Dido during registration or any of their lessons. He hated any kind of tension, because he'd been through more than enough of it in the months leading up to his parents' divorce.

When the final bell went, Philippa was on her feet and out the door like there was an emergency on somewhere.

'D'you think Philippa's ill?' Scott said to Dido.

'No, she's being stupid,' Dido snapped, thrusting books into her shoulder bag. 'All this Look-at-me-I-need-sympathy stuff is so girlie it makes me want to puke.'

Scott frowned. 'Why are you so down on her, Dido?' he said. 'It's not like you to be so mean.'

Dido blushed. Scott was absolutely right. She

hadn't meant to say what she'd said about Philippa – it seemed to have slipped out of its own accord, almost as if someone had used magic to—

But no, that couldn't be it: the only kind of witch who'd want to stir things up between friends would be a Shadowmaster, and as far as Dido was aware, the post of Stanstowe Shadowmaster was still vacant.

Maybe it's old magic left over, Dido thought.

Or maybe it was teenage mood swings.

As they were crossing the campus, Dido and Scott were joined by Ollie. Ollie obviously had something on his mind, and judging by the expression on his face it was something serious.

'Hi, Ollie!' said Scott, fumbling in his pocket for his pack of cards. 'Want to see my new trick? It's a cracker! Pick any—'

'Can you show me later, Scott?' said Ollie. 'I want to talk to Dido a minute.'

'Sure.'

'Alone,' Ollie said.

Scott frowned. Ollie and Dido were always going into secret huddles, and Scott was starting to feel left out.

'I'll see you at the bus stop,' he told Dido.

'OK, but don't wait,' said Dido. 'If the bus comes and I'm not there, go without me.'

Scott turned and slouched off, shoulders slumped.

'You've hurt his feelings,' said Ollie.

'Who, Scott? Nah!'

'He likes you a lot, you know.'

'Well of course he likes me – we're mates, aren't we? Anyway, what did you want to talk about?'

'Have you noticed anything funny going on with Philippa recently?'

'No, I haven't noticed anything funny going on with her,' said Dido. 'In fact, Philippa hasn't been funny for months.'

There it was again – a nasty comment that Dido hadn't intended to make. She hadn't even sounded like herself when she'd said it.

'I meant funny as in magic,' said Ollie. 'There's something wrong with her aura and I'm not sure what. It's like she's hiding something, or something's hiding in her.'

'When did you notice this?'

'This morning.'

'You think someone's bewitched her?'

'If they have, it's not any spell I've come across before. My hunch is that it's connected with the curse on Stanstowe.'

'But I got rid of the curse when I zapped the Shadowmaster!' said Dido.

'No you didn't,' Ollie reminded her. 'You weakened it, and it went into hibernation, but it's still there, and it's started working again. Did you read about those two teenagers who were beaten up in that club on Saturday night?'

'Yeah, but that was a drugs thing, not the curse.'

'And the kid who got hospitalised joyriding last week?'

'Coincidence.'

'Exactly!' said Ollie. 'But what's coinciding with what?'

Dido arrived home at half four. When she opened the door, she heard an unfamiliar noise that she couldn't identify at first, and she followed it through into the lounge.

Dad was stretched out on the sofa, with Cosmo curled up on his lap.

'You're watching TV!' said Dido. 'You never watch TV – especially never in the daytime.'

'I had an urge for something mindless,' said Dad. 'Anyway, technically I'm not watching.

The TV is on and I'm looking at it.'

Dad's face was strained and pale. He blinked slowly, like a tortoise.

'Tough day?' Dido asked.

Dad nodded.

'I bashed out two reviews for *Computer Digest*,' he said. 'Plus there were some other things that needed attending to.'

Now that Dido's surprise had worn off, she noticed that the house felt different, cleaner and fresher. She opened the eye of her Light Magic and went inseeing. Colours, textures, sounds and smells intensified. She seemed to be looking down on the lounge from a point on the ceiling, and a patch of late afternoon sunlight on the carpet was almost unbearably bright. The locking spells on all the doors and windows had been strengthened, and there was a new spell protecting the threshold of the sanctuary – an impressive blend of iron gates and the steel doors on bank vaults. Dad had been busy.

'Why didn't you wait for me?' said Dido.

'Before doing what?'

'Reprotecting the house. I could have given you a hand.'

'I didn't want to bother you, and I had to prove to myself that I'm more than just a techno hack.'

Dido sussed that Dad had been trying to spare her feelings. He'd renewed the spells to keep out any trespassing witches, and he hadn't wanted Dido to be alarmed.

Treating me like a kid again, Dido thought. Typical! But her anger faded as she registered the saggy skin under her father's eyes. 'You look whacked out,' she said.

'That's because I am whacked out.'

'Change of scene. Come on, let's take a drive and go for a walk in the country.'

'Dinner won't make itself,' Dad pointed out.

'It will if we order a takeaway.'

'But your mother—'

'Will understand. We'll leave her a note,' Dido said firmly. 'Get your rear in gear before you turn into a couch potato. Where would you like to go?'

'Away from exhaust fumes,' said Dad. 'What about the circle? We haven't been in a long time.'

Dido shivered and her thumbs itched. The stone circle had been the location of her showdown with the Shadowmaster, and Ollie claimed that it was the source of the Stanstowe curse.

More coincidence, Dido thought, or was her magic trying to tell her something?

'Yeah, why not?' she said quietly. 'It might help me to lay a few ghosts to rest.'

'What ghosts?' said Dad.

'In a manner of speaking,' Dido said.

The circle was on top of Stanstowe Hill, and overlooked the town. Local teenagers went there to party in the summer, and the site was scattered with litter. Some of the stones had been defaced with graffiti, which did nothing to diminish their menace.

In her mind, Dido heard the Shadowmaster shout, 'I call upon you, Spelkor, Lord of Night!' and a thought occurred to her.

'Dad,' she said, 'isn't magic supposed to come from within?'

Dad took in a breath and exhaled.

'That's right,' he said.

'Then why do Shadowmasters call on powers outside themselves?'

Dad scowled.

'How do you know that they do?' he said.

'I read it on the Internet,' Dido lied.

'Why were you surfing the Net for information on Shadow Magic?'

Dido sighed in exasperation.

'Will you stop coming the Heavy Parent and answer the question, please?' she said. 'I'm not a four-year-old any more, in case you haven't noticed. In a couple of weeks it'll be my Covening and I'll be a teenager.'

'And I'll be a teenage girl's father. I can wear baggy jeans, dance peculiarly and embarrass you in front of your friends.'

'Don't go there!' Dido warned.

But Dad was in full flow.

'D'you know what I can't wait for?' he said. 'The day your first boyfriend comes over for a meal. I'll dig out those photos we took of you when you were a baby, the ones where you're—'

'Quit trying to change the subject, Dad!' Dido snapped. 'I want to know.'

Dad relented.

'All right,' he said. 'Yes, Shadowmasters call on outside powers, the way that Light Witches call on the Goddess, but the Goddess is far more reliable. The god of Shadowmasters is a tricky customer, according to legend.'

'Is he called Spelkor?' said Dido.

Dad murmured a good-luck charm.

'Where did you get that name from?' he demanded. 'And don't say it aloud, especially here!'

'Never mind where I got the name from, who is he?'

'He's the Dark One who stole the shadows from Twilight Magic.'

'Twilight Magic?' said Dido.

'All witches were Twilight Witches once,' Dad said. 'The Dark One split Twilight Magic into Light and Shadow.' Dad's voice altered in tone as he recited from memory. *'He is the terror that walks by night and the shadow that creeps by day. He is the bringer of nightmares and chaos. He is the darkness before the beginning of time and at time's end.'*

The word 'time' rang a bell somewhere. The Shadowmaster had said that there were places outside time. Was the stone circle one of them, and why was Dad so stressed about speaking Spelkor's name aloud there?

The world went still and silent. Dad stood paralysed in mid sentence, mouth open, raised hands frozen in the air. There was no wind; the grass around the circle was motionless, and so were the clouds in the sky above it. Dido turned her eyes towards Stanstowe and it had gone. A dark forest stretched away to the hills in the distance.

Dido said, 'What's going—' A sound made her break off.

She listened to it rise and fall, like waves breaking on a shore. It was as though a vast creature was breathing deeply as it slept.

Dido didn't fancy being around when it woke up.

'I don't belong here,' she thought. 'I have to get out.'

She pictured moonlight on a stream, sunshine coming through leaves, the crackling flames of a bonfire, and...

'...but don't tell your mother I told you about the Dark One,' said Dad. 'She wouldn't approve.'

'She'd freak,' Dido said. 'Hey, Dad, are you OK?'

'Fine. It was a good idea of yours to go out.'

'You didn't notice anything weird just now?'

'Apart from my daughter's knowing a forbidden name? No. Should I have?'

'I guess not. It must have been what-d'you-call-it. You know, when you think that something's happened before?'

'Déjà vu,' said Dad. 'That's French for "already seen".'

'I hope not,' Dido whispered; then she said, 'Can we go? The circle doesn't like me.'

'Don't you mean that you don't like it?'

'I know what I mean,' Dido said.

Mum was in by the time that Dido and Dad got back.

'Enjoy the walk?' she said.

'Yes,' said Dad. 'But it wasn't my fault. Dido bullied me.'

'So would you if you'd seen him, Mum,' Dido said. 'He looked like he was about to come down with cabin fever.'

'Where did you go?' Mum asked.

'The circle,' said Dad.

Mum beamed. 'I love it there,' she said. 'It's the one spot in Stanstowe that I'd describe as tranquil.'

Which was exactly the word that Dido wouldn't have used. Her parents evidently didn't sense what she sensed at the circle.

Maybe I'm the only one, Dido thought. Maybe it's tuned in to me.

'What were you going to ask me this morning?' Mum said to Dido.

'No worries. It was a magic thing. Dad sorted me out.'

'Did I?' said Dad; then, when he caught the glance that Dido gave him, he added, 'Oh yes, that's right, I did!'

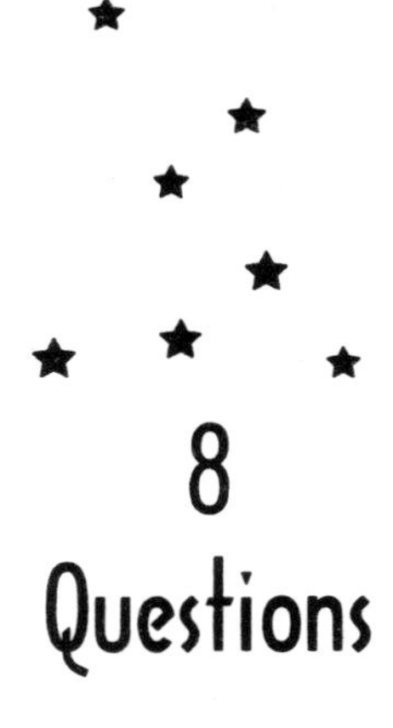

8
Questions

For the next few days, Zinny occupied most of Philippa's thoughts. She tried to picture what Zinny looked like: what kind of face would fit the sparky personality that had come over the chatline? Philippa started with the bits of Zinny that she knew – straight mousy hair, dental brace – and let her imagination fill in the rest.

Zinny was tall and lanky, clumsy in her movements. Her face was heart-shaped, with a snub nose and freckled cheeks. Her eyes were round and grey, and she wore spectacles with outrageous flamingo-pink frames. She smiled a lot, but clamped her lips tight when she remembered her brace. When she talked, she pulled lots of different expressions and waved her arms around so that she was all elbows and fingers. At school, she wore a white blouse and a tartan skirt, like the high-school girls in American soaps. After school, Zinny changed into her real clothes: jeans, baggy sweatshirt and trainers with flashing lights in the heels. She was funny, happy-go-lucky and up for anything – just the sort of person Philippa wished that she could be herself.

But there were mysteries surrounding Zinny. Why was she so cagey about where she lived, and why would she get into trouble for being on-line? *Families suck, don't they?* Perhaps Zinny had said it because her parents were strict with her.

Philippa wanted answers; she had to know. She hoped that Zinny called back soon.

At breakfast on Friday, Tom was a major pain. He was taking pictures with the digital camera, and caught Philippa unawares when she walked into the dining room. He tried to snap her again, but backed off when she growled, 'Tom, get that thing out of my face or lose a limb!'

'Don't you want to be a supermodel?' said Tom.

'Not if I have to be photographed by irritating little squirts like you.'

'Grouch!'

'Nerd.'

'Poo brain!'

'Anorak.'

Tom frowned for a word and came out with, 'Trottle-nobbler!'

Philippa couldn't keep from laughing.

'What's a trottle-nobbler?' she said.

'Don't know. I just made it up – yes I do! It's what you are.'

Alison appeared in the doorway, holding a plate of toast.

Tom pointed the camera at her. 'Say cheese!'

Alison did more than say cheese: she cocked her head on one side, lifted her left foot behind her and flashed a dazzling grin. Tom went on taking pictures as Alison struck pose after pose, until they both had a fit of giggles.

Look at her! thought Philippa. Is she a show-off or what? Mum would never have done anything like that, she hated having her photo taken.

'You shouldn't fool around with the camera like that, Tom,' Philippa said. 'It isn't a toy, you know.'

Tom's giggles got worse and so did Alison's.

'Did I say something funny?' Philippa asked.

Alison managed to control herself. 'I'm sorry, Philippa,' she said, 'but you sounded like a little old lady telling off her grandson.'

'No she didn't!' Tom hooted. 'She sounded like a trottle-nobbler!'

It set Alison off again.

Philippa thought that they might as well have a fence around them with a notice saying: Keep Out.

Dad entered the dining room, saw Tom and Alison laughing together and his eyes went soft, the way they used to sometimes when he looked at Mum.

Philippa didn't know why it hurt her, but the pain made her feel sick.

I don't want to be here, she thought. I don't want to do this. Help!

Zinny: she'd tell Zinny about it; Zinny would understand.

At the end of school, Philippa went straight home. Alison was in the garden, in a deckchair. An opened file lay on her lap and she was talking to someone on her mobile, using the posh phone voice that set Philippa's teeth on edge. Tom was in the lounge, seated in front of the computer, so into it that he didn't notice Philippa.

Philippa went over to see what he was doing.

The picture that Tom had taken of Philippa at breakfast was on the monitor. Tom had altered it so that Philippa had green skin, blue hair and orange eyes. She looked like an alien monster.

'Thanks a lot, Tom!'

Tom jumped a few centimetres into the air.

'Er, I was just messing about with the photo thing!' he gabbled.

'I notice it's my picture you're messing around with, not one of Alison.'

Tom blushed.

'Only because your picture came first,' he said.

Philippa wasn't convinced, but let it drop because she needed some information.

'D'you ever get onto chatlines?' she said.

'Only all the time! I'm Surferdude. Have you got a Net name yet?'

'Storme. With an "e".'

Tom sniggered, and stifled it.

'Have you ever chatted with someone called Zinny?' said Philippa.

'Jenny?'

'No, Zinny.'

Philippa spelt it out for him.

Tom shook his head. 'Never heard of her.'

'I chatted to her the other day. She's American.'

'My best Net buddy's in Australia.'

'Isn't it strange to be friends with someone who lives on the other side of the world?'

'Yes, but it's safer. You don't know who you're chatting to on the Net. If it's someone who lives locally, you could end up being stalked by some perv.'

Philippa hadn't thought of that. Zinny could be anybody, pretending to be a friendly teenage girl. She might even be a dirty old man.

'How can you tell, Tom?'

'You can't. Don't give anyone your home address, and if anyone ever tries to set up a meeting, don't go. Keep the fun in Cyberspace.'

'But Cyberspace isn't real, is it?'

'Hey!' said Tom. 'I'm ten. What do I know about reality?'

'Are you going to be much longer? I want to get on to the Net.'

Tom closed down the picture and slid off the chair. 'All yours!' he said, and left the room to go thundering upstairs to his bedroom.

Philippa opened the Internet file and read through the chatline's home page menu. She didn't have to wait for long.

Howdy doody, Storme!! How's tricks?

Not so hot.

How come?

My friends aren't talking to me.

What's the story?

We sort of fell out at the beginning of the week. I said some stuff I didn't mean.

So tell them you're sorry.

Why should I? It wasn't my fault.

Oh no?

Only a bit. I was in a bad mood.

And you took it out on them, huh? You shouldn't do that, you know? You wind up hurting yourself.

My family's no help.

Tell me more.

This morning my kid brother Tom and Alison were laughing about something, and then my Dad came in and they were...

What?

Happy. I felt left out.

Lighten up, will ya? The world's not gonna stop because your mom isn't in it any more. Your dad and your kid brother have put the past behind them so they can get on with their lives. That doesn't mean they don't care about your mom.

Doesn't it?

No way!!! Think your mom would expect everybody

to shut themselves away and be sad?

I suppose not. Zinny, how old are you?

Thirteen. I told you already.

You sound more grown up than that.

I'm very mature for my age - in some ways. About other stuff, I'm a regular kid.

What stuff?

I'm crazy for that band Boys-4-U. You know them? Every time I see their picture in a magazine, I totally flip!!

But they broke up last year.

They did?

The lead singer went solo.

Marty Rowan?

His CD sold millions. I can't believe you didn't know about it.

Guess I must be out of touch. News takes a long time to reach where I am.

You make it sound like the back of beyond.

How d'you guess?

Are you at the South Pole?

It's cold, but the South Pole it ain't.

Where is it then?

I'm not supposed to say.

Why not?

I'm not supposed to say that either.

Is it a secret?

Kinda.

Are your parents spies or something?

ROFL. Not even close, Storme!!!

Then why is it a secret?

Can't stay. Someone's expecting me. Will you do something for me?

What?

Don't forget about me when I'm not there. Bye!!

Philippa had only asked a few of the questions she'd meant to ask, and now she had even more questions. Was Zinny telling the truth, or was she making stuff up to make herself more interesting?

Philippa thought about Zinny so much that she didn't notice she'd stopped thinking about herself.

The keyboard and monitor disappeared so fast that Zinny said, 'H-e-e-y!'

She was seated on a stool in front of a stainless steel counter. The man was behind the counter, wearing a chef's hat and a purple apron.

'I wish things wouldn't do that!' Zinny grumbled.

'Do what?'

'Change like that.'

'Would you prefer that everything remained the same?'

said the man. 'That might become rather tedious, might it not? This is a world of infinite possibilities. You should enjoy them.'

'I do, but I wish you'd give me a warning or something. So...how am I doing?'

'Well,' said the man. 'Storme has confided in you sooner than I dared hope.'

'That's because we're both lonesome,' said Zinny. 'What's the deal with Storme, anyhow? How come you're so interested in her – you some kind of relative of hers?'

The man smiled evasively.

'We have mutual acquaintances,' he said. 'I always take a keen interest in the lonely. I find them more suggestible.'

'Say what?'

'Open to persuasion,' said the man. 'Now, what is your pleasure?'

'Huh?'

The man gestured to indicate the chrome faucets and glass shelving on his side of the bar. The shelves were stacked with candy bars, cakes, cookies and Danish pastries; the faucets were tagged with every brand of soda that Zinny had ever heard of.

'Something to eat, perhaps?' the man said.

'Sure! A triple scoop of pistachio ice cream with

bananas and hot chocolate fudge sauce.'

Almost before Zinny had finished speaking, the ice cream appeared in front of her in a cut-glass dish, steam curling from the sauce. Beside the dish was a spoon wrapped in a paper napkin. Zinny took the spoon and cautiously prodded the ice cream.

'Is this for real?' she said.

'Not real in the strictest sense of the word,' said the man. 'But how does it taste?'

Zinny tried a tiny bit.

'Delicious!' she said, and put a whole spoonful in her mouth.

'Then it is real enough,' said the man. 'Here, anything you desire is real – and it is all free.'

Zinny eyed the man suspiciously.

'My dad always says that nothing comes for free,' she said.

'Your father displayed admirable wisdom,' the man said with a shrug, 'but in this world, that wisdom no longer applies.'

9
Memories

As Alice Morgan closed the door of her flat, she suddenly realised that she couldn't recall a single detail of her drive home. Shocked at herself, she leaned back against the door and willed herself to remember: at the end of school she'd gone to the staff room, spoken to the student teacher who was working in the Drama department, and then – but no, that had been earlier in the week. Everything between the ringing of the final bell and her putting her key into the lock was a complete blank. Alice was dismayed: traffic was always heavier on Fridays and she'd driven the whole complex journey, with its cyclists, roundabouts, T-junctions and Pelican crossings on autopilot.

You're not fit to be out! she murmured to herself. *You're a car smash waiting to happen.*

What could she have been thinking of – and

where had her mind been while her body was behind the wheel?

No, Alice said aloud. Don't even think about it.

She was tired, that was all. Every Drama lesson she taught was a performance, fuelled by adrenalin. Now, at the end of the week, her adrenalin had run out and she felt all her weight pressing on the soles of her feet. She could do with pampering, and since there was no one to do it for her, she'd have to pamper herself.

A long bath, a pizza delivery and a veg-out in front of the TV, she thought. And perhaps she'd open the bottle of wine that she'd been saving for a special occasion.

Alice went through into the lounge. Normally she was glad to be at home – the flat was a haven of calm after the chaos of teaching – but today the place depressed her. She surveyed the room as though she were a stranger: a table and two dining chairs, an armchair and a settee, a shelf of books from her student days and a television set on top of a tacky sideboard. The only brightness in the room was a poster advertising a production of *Hamlet* that she'd once seen in Stratford, and that was starting to fade.

The doors that led into the kitchen and bathroom were open, reminding Alice that she'd left her breakfast dishes in the sink and her bed unmade. Well, it wouldn't hurt to leave them a while longer. She flopped on to the settee, dug the remote out from behind a cushion, pointed it at the television and pressed the power button. She wanted to hear voices – any voices except the ones in her head, the ones that told her she was lonely and wasting her life.

What had gone wrong? Alice had made plenty of friends at university, and some close friends who still kept in touch, but they were scattered around the country and never seemed to have the time to visit her. She'd had boyfriends too, nothing serious, but since moving to Stanstowe three years previously, her social life had dwindled to nothing. Embarrassment still made her toes curl when she thought of the night she'd gone clubbing, and an A-level student from Prince Arthur's had attempted to chat her up. After that, she hardly ever went out. There was an atmosphere about Stanstowe at night, a dangerous edginess that made her feel threatened. All she did was work, eat, sleep and go back to work.

Alice had lost count of the number of times she'd made up her mind to resign her post and make a fresh start in a new town. On more than one occasion she'd stood outside the Head's door with her letter of resignation at the ready, but she hadn't been able to bring herself to hand it in. It was as if Stanstowe had a hold over her that she couldn't break.

The television tuned itself in to a children's news programme that Alice hadn't come across before. The presenter was striking – a tall man with a hooked nose, a pointed chin, and high cheekbones. The studio lighting was peculiar, a dark purple that gave Alice the impression that the picture was somehow bigger than the screen.

'And finally, a special report,' said the presenter. 'To you, she is Miss, just another teacher at your school, but have you ever stopped to think that teachers are people? They have the same dreams and disappointments as we all do.'

His voice was deep and soothing; his dark, slightly bulging eyes were so compelling that Alice couldn't look away.

'This particular teacher entered her profession with high hopes,' the presenter continued. 'She wanted to inspire young people, make them see the world differently. Unfortunately, these hopes are as yet unfulfilled, but it is not too late, Alice.'

Alice wasn't alarmed that the presenter was talking directly to her; his tone was warm and sympathetic.

'Isn't it?' she said.

'Far from it. You have much to give, if you make proper use of your talents.'

'Talents?'

The presenter smiled.

'Come now, Alice, you know exactly what I mean,' he said. 'We are both aware that all your life you have resisted the power that lies inside you. You have constantly denied your true self. Why is that, I wonder?'

'I'm afraid,' said Alice. 'Sometimes my thoughts are so wild, I think I must be going mad.'

The presenter shook his head.

'Fear is foolish, Alice,' he said. 'It holds you back from accepting who you really are. Once you learn to do that, you will find happiness.'

'But how do I go about accepting who I really am?'

'I can show you. Listen to me and listen carefully. You have spent too long struggling against yourself alone. I've seen your light flying through the darkness, searching for a home. But you searched in the wrong place, Alice. I will send you a companion, a guide who will lead you to enlightenment...'

The presenter's voice washed over Alice, flooding her mind. Her muscles slackened and her eyelids began to droop.

She woke with a start and blinked at the television screen. Top of the Pops was on; she must have slept for almost three hours. Alice turned off the television and yawned. She felt refreshed and sharp – a snooze had been just what she needed. She tried to recollect the strange dream she'd had, but it slipped away: probably just as well, her dreams didn't make much sense anyway, particularly the ones she'd been having recently.

For the next half hour, Alice soaked herself in a hot bath laced with aromatherapy oils and they worked; when she got out, she was more relaxed than she'd been for ages. She wrapped her damp hair in a towel, pulled on a bath robe, went into the lounge to phone for a pizza, then headed for the bedroom to dress before the delivery man arrived.

A sound made her stop, a scrabbling that made her think that there might be mice in the flat – but the sound was too loud for mice, surely?

Frowning curiously, Alice followed the scrabbling into the hall.

The noise was coming from the front door.

A glance through the peep-hole revealed nothing more than the empty landing outside.

Alice slotted the security chain in place and cautiously opened the door.

A shape slipped through the narrow gap.

Alice couldn't be sure what she was seeing at first. For a moment she glimpsed a mass of bedraggled fur, and then her vision cleared. A silver tabby cat was rubbing itself against her legs, arching its back and purring.

Alice was delighted: the spot she'd always had for cats wasn't so much soft as gooey.

'Hello, you handsome beast! Where have you sprung from, eh?'

She stroked the silky head, and the cat rolled over on to its back to have its stomach scratched. Alice found the invitation irresistible; the touch of her hand made the cat purr ecstatically.

There was a collar around the animal's neck, with a small metal cylinder attached.

Alice unscrewed the cylinder and took out the small roll of paper inside.

'Let's see who you belong to,' she said. 'Whoever it is, I'm jealous of them.'

Malkin
Flat 6B Prentice Court,
Dee Road,
Stanstowe,
ST13 6AB

'But that's here!' gasped Alice. 'That's my address. How did—'

The cat mewed insistently.

'Yes,' said Alice. 'Of course. I'll see to it right away.'

There was a Buy-Rite supermarket on the corner that stayed open till late. If she dressed quickly she could go there, buy cat food and be back before her pizza arrived.

'Malkin,' Alice said softly, running her fingers through the cat's coat.

Funny, she'd promised herself that one day she'd have a cat called Malkin.

A stream of memories flowed through her head: Malkin as a kitten, chasing a ping-pong ball; Malkin clambering up her back and on to her shoulder as she did the washing up; Malkin stretched out on the windowsill above the double radiator.

The fact that the memories were false didn't bother Alice in the least; by the time she left the flat on her way to the supermarket, she was convinced that she and Malkin had been together for years.

10
The Distractor

Dido gave in to her lazy, Saturday-morning feeling and lay on her back, looking up at the bedroom ceiling. She thought over what Ollie had told her about Philippa, but somehow that turned into thinking about Ollie.

Ollie was the closest friend Dido had ever had. Being able to discuss her magic with someone who really understood, as Ollie did, was a relief and a comfort, and he knew her better than anyone else – including her parents. She'd told him all about her battle with the Shadowmaster and her experiments with Shadow Magic, things she had to keep hidden from Mum and Dad. Ollie was a good mate, and because his second sight enabled him to see things that Dido couldn't, they made a good team, but just recently Dido had caught herself wondering what it would be like if she and Ollie were more than mates.

The trouble was, Ollie obviously didn't wonder the same thing. He was interested in Dido, but only because she was a witch, not because she was a girl.

This was new territory for Dido and she found it bewildering; she was also annoyed with herself.

'I don't *do* the girl-boy thing!' she murmured.

At the sound of Dido's voice, Cosmo, who'd been sleeping at the foot of the bed, came marching up the duvet and plonked herself on Dido's chest.

'Cosmo,' said Dido, 'is there a spell I could cast to stop myself turning into a total airhead?'

Cosmo replied that it was a well-established fact that if you were in doubt about anything, feeding your cat always helped.

'OK, OK!' Dido said with a laugh. 'I can take a hint.'

Mum was in the kitchen, gazing absently out of the window at the back garden while she waited for the coffee machine to finish doing its stuff.

Cosmo jumped on to the work surface and Dido, obeying Cosmo's instructions, took a sachet of chicken and giblets cat food from the cupboard next to the washing machine.

'We feed that cat far too often,' Mum said. 'She's getting positively tubby.'

Cosmo let out an offended growl.

'What's all the noise about?' said Mum.

'She wants to know where you get off passing personal remarks,' Dido said. 'Hey, Mum, remember that guy you told me about, the one you had the crush on? How does that work? I mean, what's it like to have a crush?'

Mum frowned.

'Are we talking theoretically, or practically?' she said.

'Kind of for future reference.'

Mum's frown relaxed.

'It's delicious agony,' she said. 'When you have a crush on somebody, you can't stop thinking about them, even when you don't want to. They're in your thoughts from the time you wake up until the time you go to bed, and when you're asleep you dream about them. You're convinced that every love song you hear was written for you.'

'Oh,' said Dido, remembering the tracks she'd been listening to on her personal stereo. 'Where does the agony come in?'

'That was a bit of an exaggeration,' Mum confessed. 'It's more a sort of dull ache, like you're about to go down with flu.'

'Sounds fun!' Dido said sarcastically.

'It is, particularly when the person you have a crush on doesn't feel the same about you.'

'Excuse me?'

'You imagine what the relationship would be like, even though it makes you miserable. I used to stare into the mirror a lot to see what my face looked like when I was in love.'

Dido didn't get it.

'Isn't that wallowing in self pity?' she said.

'Exactly, and there's nothing to beat it,' Mum said. 'You'll understand when it happens to you.'

Dido sighed: she'd hoped that talking to Mum would help to sort things out; instead it had only confirmed her worst suspicions.

'Depressing, isn't it?' she said.

'What is?'

'Growing up.'

And, to cap it all, Mum said, 'I don't think you ever do grow up. You just get bigger and older.'

Dido's Saturday routine included catching the bus into town after lunch, meeting up with Philippa and Ollie, and hanging out. Sometimes Scott joined them, but not often.

That Saturday, Ollie was at the usual rendezvous point – the bench next to the statue of Queen Victoria that stood outside the Town Hall – but Philippa wasn't.

Ollie and Dido waited for her, chatting about nothing in particular, and then Dido heard the Town Hall clock chime half past two.

'It doesn't look like Philippa's going to show,' she said.

'No, it doesn't,' Ollie agreed.

'I guess we've got ourselves to each other. Where shall we go?'

Ollie had grown increasingly uncomfortable, and now he wriggled his shoulders as if someone had dropped an ice cube down the back of his sweatshirt.

'Maybe we should...' he said. 'Don't you think we ought to...'

'Spit it out, Ollie!'

'Er...aren't you worried?'

'About?'

Ollie took a deep breath and said, 'Well, if people see the two of us together, they might think that we're dating or something.'

He made it sound as appealing as being hit by an articulated truck.

Dido's heart sank.

'Let people think what they want,' she said gruffly. 'I'm not bothered.'

'Fine! I just didn't want anyone to get the wrong impression about us, that's all.'

'As if!' Dido said.

Town was seething. Everywhere Dido looked, there were signs of trouble brewing: groups of teenagers jeering at one another; young boys in tracksuits chucking twists of paper that made a snapping sound when they hit the ground; two drunks having a loud argument in a shop doorway.

'Why is everybody so stroppy today?' said Dido.

'I think the curse is flexing its muscles,' Ollie said grimly. 'Let's find somewhere quiet.'

To get somewhere quiet, Dido and Ollie had to join the crowds that filed into the Pentacle, Stanstowe's huge shopping mall. The symbol of the Pentacle – a five-pointed star – was plastered over everything. It seemed no coincidence to Dido that a five-pointed star was also the symbol of Shadow Magic. She had a hunch that it had something to do with the curse on the town, but so far she hadn't been able to make a direct connection.

Once they were inside the Pentacle, Dido and

Ollie entered the relative peace of Springers' bookshop, and made their way to the snack bar inside. Dido bought a fizzy mineral water and one of the giant chocolate-chip cookies that she suspected were addictive; Ollie had a cappuccino. They found an empty table and sat down.

Ollie was quieter without Philippa around, and he had something on his mind; Dido could feel him holding himself back.

'What's up, Ollie?' she said. 'Are you embarrassed at being with me like this?'

'No, it's Philippa,' said Ollie. 'I'm worried about her.'

Philippa again; even when she wasn't there she managed to get in the way.

Dido suppressed a hot surge of anger and said, 'Want to talk about it?'

This seemed to give Ollie the cue he'd been waiting for, and he suddenly became talkative again.

'It's more than just her dad getting remarried,' he said. 'They're only little things, but when you put them all together...'

'For instance?'

'First there's that thing in her aura, then there's the way she avoids everybody.'

'She doesn't avoid you,' Dido pointed out.

Ollie shrugged with one shoulder.

'Talking to me is just a habit she's got into,' he said. 'But what really worries me is that she rang me last night and went on and on about this friend she's made on the Internet – Zinny. It was Zinny this and Zinny that, and her voice was weird – like sing-song? She sounded as if she was reading from a script and...well, she wasn't Philippa.'

Dido's anger was getting out of control. She wanted to grab Ollie's coffee cup and smash it.

'You have a thing for Philippa, don't you?' she said.

The effect was dramatic. Ollie recoiled in his chair, bumping the table so that coffee slopped into his saucer.

'What's up?' Dido said, startled by Ollie's reaction.

Ollie's face was pale.

'I just second-sighted you,' he said, 'and something moved in your eyes.'

'What something?'

'Something magic.'

And all at once Dido knew why she'd been overreacting to Philippa. If she hadn't been so busy eating her heart out over Ollie, she would have spotted it straightaway: the anger she felt wasn't her own; it was an intruder.

Her reflexes kicked in, turning her inseeing eye on herself.

Self-inseeing was one of the trickiest things a Light Witch could attempt. It took considerable delicacy and patience – neither of which were among Dido's strong points – but she remembered all the training she'd had from her parents and plunged in.

The snack bar vanished like a drawing torn out of a sketchbook. Dido was gliding above the surface of a still, dark ocean. Above her, the sky was white and featureless. Far off to her left, at the edge of the horizon, hung a minute speck that she knew didn't belong. She turned towards it, thought of rockets and downhill skiers, and felt a wind ruffle her hair as she picked up speed.

The speck grew larger. It wavered from side to side as though uncertain of what to do, then fell towards the water. Intuition told Dido that if she didn't reach it before it broke the surface, it would be lost forever. She power-dived. Her arms sprouted feathers; her face pushed itself forward into a hooked yellow bill; the skin on her hands wrinkled, their fingernails turned into black talons. Dido extended them, and the shock of the strike jarred right through her...

She was in the snack bar again. Ollie was staring at the table, his nose wrinkled in disgust. Dido looked down.

She'd caught a Shadow Magic spell, an ugly little thing that was a cross between a slug and a centipede. Its wounded body writhed and its legs rippled as they scrabbled to get a grip on the table's shiny surface. The spell opened its pincer-like jaws and made a sound like a marble rattling in a cardboard tube.

Dido didn't know what she should do next, but her Shadow Magic did. It produced a spell in the form of a long curved blade that scythed through the slug-centipede again and again, chopping it into pieces, then atoms, then nothingness. The blade and the Shadow spell vanished at the same time.

'What,' Ollie said slowly, 'was *that*?'

'It's known in the witch biz as a distractor,' said Dido. 'They mess with people's heads. They take negative emotions and magnify them until the victim can't tell what day of the week it is.'

'Is it a Shadow Magic thing?' Ollie asked.

Dido nodded.

'But there isn't a Shadowmaster in Stanstowe any more, is there?' Ollie said. 'You told me that you got rid of him.'

'I did,' said Dido.

'Then where did the distractor come from, and why was it trying to distract *you*?'

'Excellent questions,' said Dido. 'I only wish I could think of some excellent answers.'

11
Outsiders

This time, Zinny was seated in a high-backed chair in the foyer of a swanky hotel – all dark wood panelling and crystal chandeliers. The upholstery, carpets and curtains were the same shade of lavender. The man was there too, wearing a bellhop's uniform that matched the fittings; his pillbox hat was set at a jaunty angle.

He smiled and said, 'Check your luggage, lady?'

'Cut it out!' snorted Zinny. 'I don't have any luggage. You know I don't. And that has to be the worst American accent I've ever heard.'

The man pursed his lips.

'I was attempting to enter into the spirit of things – which you evidently are not,' he said. 'This hotel has many luxuriously appointed suites, any one of which is yours for the asking.'

Zinny gave the man a sour look.

'But no other guests, right?' she said.

'Regrettably, the resources of the hotel can only stretch so far. What kind of accommodation do you require?'

Zinny sulked and kicked her legs.

'I don't want a room, I want information,' she said.

'Upon what topic?'

'Storme.'

'Ah, Storme! Of course. What would you like to know?'

'Everything.'

The man laughed.

'To explain everything would take more time than we have at our disposal,' he said. 'You must be more specific.'

'Why d'you want me to contact her?'

'You find it unpleasant?'

'No!' said Zinny. The man was twisting her words around, the way he always did. 'I like Storme. She's my friend.'

'As you are hers, and Storme is in need of a friend at present.'

'Why?'

The man plucked an invisible hair from the shoulder of his uniform.

'She has what you would call unresolved issues concerning her mother's demise,' he said.

'Huh?'

'She is still grieving, and you can help her.'

'By getting her to achieve closure?'

'That is not my primary concern,' the man said. 'It is necessary for Storme to be occupied, and you are the one I have chosen to occupy her.'

'And if I say no?'

The man's face darkened. He seemed to grow taller and his shoulders widened. A brass button popped off his uniform and bounced across the deep-piled carpet.

'Then I shall take all this away and send you into the black nothing where you belong,' he said.

Zinny shrugged with her mouth and said, 'I guess that means I won't be saying "no".'

Philippa deliberately stayed in bed late. She heard Dad and Alison go downstairs into the kitchen; Tom followed them ten minutes later. The smell of frying bacon wafted through the house, so Philippa guessed that Dad was making bacon sandwiches. Her stomach gurgled hungrily, but she was determined not to give in. She thought of the thick layer of peanut butter that Alison would spread on her sandwich. Tom had tried it too and said that it tasted great, but Philippa couldn't bring herself to eat something that looked so disgusting.

At eleven o' clock, Tom tapped on the door and barged in.

'Aren't you up yet?' he said. 'We're all ready to go to the supermarket.'

'Then go,' said Philippa.

'Aren't you coming?'

'No. I don't feel very well,' Philippa lied.

'Yeah, right,' said Tom.

Philippa sat up and glared at him.

'You shouldn't be in this room!' she snapped. 'This is my private space. It's out of bounds!'

'Keep your wig on, grumpy!'

Tom stepped back on to the landing, closed the door and ran downstairs, making a noise like a small avalanche.

Heavier footsteps climbed the stairs – Dad. Philippa ducked her head under the duvet and pretended to be asleep.

'Philippa?'

'Mmm?'

'Tom says that you're not feeling well.'

'It's only a headache,' Philippa said, keeping her voice feeble. 'I'll be OK, but I can't face the supermarket.'

'Shall I get you an aspirin?'

'I'll take one later.'

'Shall I stay with you? I don't like the idea of your being in on your own.'

Philippa felt guilty about lying, and the guilt made her cross.

'For goodness' sake, Dad, I'll be all right!' she said. 'I'm not a baby.'

This was when Dad should have said something about how if she wasn't a baby, she should stop behaving like one, but instead he retreated.

Philippa waited until she heard the car reverse on to the street, then got up. She made herself a mug of tea, carried it and a bowl of cereal into the lounge, sat down at the computer and logged on.

The Chatline box came on screen almost immediately.

What's happening with you, Storme?

I've got the house to myself. Dad, Tom and Alison have gone shopping.

What day is it with you?

Philippa thought this was a strange question.

Saturday. What day is it where you are?

Saturday, huh? Big day. Guess you'll be meeting up with your friends.

I'm not in the mood. How about you and your friends? You must have loads.

Uh uh! Count 'em - zilch!!

How come?

This place. No visitors. No time off for good behaviour.

The skin at the back of Philippa's neck tingled.

Zinny, are you in prison?

LOL!!! I wish! I could talk to the other prisoners if I was in jail.

Are you in hospital? Have you been ill?

Kinda. I'm recuperating from something.

Was it something serious?

It took Zinny a while to respond.

It's difficult for me to explain it in a way that you'd understand, Storme. Also I don't feel much like going into it, because it bores my buns off!! I'd rather find out stuff about you.

Philippa sensed that Zinny was trying to put her off and decided to press her.

You know lots about me, but I hardly know anything about you. What do you look like?

Why would you want to know that?

Just curious.

The most important part of me is right there on your screen, Storme. The rest doesn't matter. Let's agree

that I look exactly like you think I look and leave it at that, deal?

Do I have a choice?

Nope, so live with it. How's Alison?

Still around.

Wish she wasn't?

Too right! Any suggestions on how I can get rid of her?

Which Alison d'you want to get rid of?

Sorry, I don't understand the question.

Seems to me you've got two Alisons. There's like regular Alison, and then there's the Alison in your head - the stepmom from Hell!!!

I only have to put up with it for three more years. I'll be sixteen then. I can leave home.

Didn't you do that already?

I don't get you.

Alison has a home, she lives there with your dad and your kid bro, but not you, Storme. You don't fit in. You've turned yourself into an outsider. Outside isn't a happy place to be.

I wouldn't be an outsider if Alison went away. Things would go back to normal.

ROFL!!! Don't bet on it. Normal isn't normal any more, because everything changed when your mom died.

Maybe, but things would be better without Alison.

You might think so, but what about your dad and Tom? They're part of what's normal, aren't they? If they were sad because they missed Alison, you wouldn't be happy either. Mind if I tell you something?

If you like.

No, I don't like, but you need to hear it. I warn you, it's pretty personal.

I thought it might be.

Ready? Here goes!! You're unbelievably selfish, Storme.

Philippa felt a sting of anger.

Selfish? What gives you the right to call me selfish?

Because it's true and friends ought to tell each other the truth, even if it hurts. You're so wrapped up in the way you wish things were, you've forgotten how lucky you are.

Lucky?!

Sure you're lucky - wise up!! You have a family, friends, a future to look forward to. Not everybody has those things. Try thinking about somebody other than yourself.

Hey, give it to me straight, Zinny! Don't hold back or anything, will you?

You mad at me?

Not exactly.

Miffed?

Yeah, but I'll get over it.

Guess you will at that. I'm outta time - bye-ee!!

The Chatline box vanished, but Philippa went on staring at the screen. Zinny had given her a lot to think about. Philippa saw herself as the guardian of her mother's memory – but how did the rest of her family see her?

Philippa wasn't really sure that she wanted to know.

The car pulled into the drive at one o'clock. A rear door flew open, and Tom came charging into the house.

'We're going to Chessington World of Adventure!' he announced excitedly.

'When?' said Philippa.

'Tomorrow,' Tom said, and charged out again.

Must be Alison's idea, thought Philippa. Give the children a fun day so she can make-believe happy families. She'll even scream when the white-knuckle ride loops the loop, to show Dad that she's a big kid at heart.

She went into the kitchen, where Dad, Tom and Alison were putting away the shopping.

'How's the headache?' Dad asked.

'Getting better,' said Philippa.

'Has Tom told you about tomorrow?'

'Yes.'

'What do you think?'

Philippa had been saving her next move; now the time seemed right to use it.

'Actually, I wanted to go to the crematorium tomorrow and visit Mum at the Garden of Remembrance,' she said. 'I haven't been for ages.'

Dad's head jerked back as if he'd been slapped and a muscle twitched in his jaw.

'Why does she always spoil everything?' Tom whined.

Philippa looked Alison straight in the eyes and thought, Get out of that one!'

And to Philippa's amazement, Alison did.

'No problem,' Alison said smoothly. 'Nothing's going to be spoiled. Tom and your dad can go to Chessington, and I'll drive you to the crematorium.'

It wasn't what Philippa had planned. She'd pictured herself, Dad and Tom at the Garden of Remembrance while Alison waited at home, or in the car.

Dad said, 'There's no need for you to bother, Alison. I'll take Philippa.'

Alison smiled.

'It's no bother,' she said. 'You and Tom have the company car, I'll use the runaround.'

Philippa had the uneasy feeling that she'd been outmanoeuvred. She didn't want to be alone with Alison, but it was too late to back down.

'All right,' she said. 'Thank you, Alison.' She made 'thank you' sound like 'get lost'.

'Are you sure, Alison?' said Dad. 'Because I can always—'

'I'm sure,' Alison said. 'We both are, aren't we, Philippa?'

And Philippa said the only thing she could say, which was, 'Yes.'

12
Into the Magic

When Dido woke on Sunday morning, questions were circling in her mind like a flock of roosting starlings. Where had the distractor come from, and why hadn't she been aware of it until Ollie pointed it out? What was going on between her and Philippa – was their friendship really falling apart, or was Shadow Magic stirring things up? And the million-pound question: how could Shadow Magic be working without a Shadowmaster?

Dido wished that she could spare the time to find some answers, but she couldn't; Sunday mornings were strictly for homework, and this Sunday she had a bagful.

Dido got stuck in right after breakfast, and didn't emerge from her bedroom until lunchtime. After lunch it was straight on to magic lessons with Dad. They went into the lounge and Dad turned on the lamp that stood on the side table next to the sofa.

'We're going to explore the interaction between magic and electromagnetic systems,' he said.

'We're going to explore *what?*' Dido yelped.

'Magic and electricity are both forms of energy and they both obey rules,' Dad explained, 'except you won't find the rules of magic written down in a science textbook. If you apply magic carefully, you can affect electrical machinery.'

'What – like computers and supermarket checkout tills?' said Dido, racing ahead. 'That would be cool! Think of all the money you could save if—'

'Dido,' Dad interrupted, 'slow down. For one thing, computers and cash tills are extraordinarily complex, and for another, I wouldn't want you to use your magic irresponsibly. We'll start with a simple machine – this lamp.'

'A lamp is a machine?'

'Yes, it makes light. I'm going to show you how to turn it on and off.'

'I already know, Dad!' Dido protested. 'See, on the side there's this little piece of plastic called a switch. What you have to do is—'

'With magic,' Dad said patiently.

'What's the point? It's a waste of time. Isn't it easier just to use the switch?'

'The point is, you haven't used magic to do this before. Once you've mastered it, we'll progress to something more difficult.'

'Like what – a fridge?'

'Look,' Dad said, 'let's make an agreement. You bear with me, and I'll bear with you, all right? Then we might get through the afternoon without having a row.'

Dido relented. She and Dad were like the Hare and the Tortoise in the old fable: Dad liked to take things slow and steady; Dido was inclined to charge in with all guns blazing.

'All right, Dads,' she said. 'We'll do it like you say.'

'Good! Now sit on the sofa, and when you're ready, insee the lamp. Try to get inside it.'

'How can you tell when you're inside a lamp?'

'You'll experience it through invision. What you'll see depends on how your magic reacts.'

'What do you see?'

'I'm not telling,' said Dad. 'Every witch sees it in his or her own way.'

As Dido applied inseeing, she couldn't resist adding a mild unlocking spell. It was only a mixture of opening milk cartons and popping champagne corks, but it made the lampshade quiver.

'Hoi, no cheating!' said Dad. 'Be gentle.'

Dido removed the spell and thought of deep places – caves and mineshafts.

The body of the lamp seemed to expand and swallow her, and all at once she was inside.

She saw an endless line of people shuffling in single file along a dark tunnel. Hidden speakers issued a stream of instructions that echoed off the tunnel walls.

'Move along there! Stay in line! Keep moving! No pushing, no dawdling!'

Dido followed the flow until she reached a massive iron gate, open wide enough to admit one person at a time. Beside the gate stood a squat little man wearing brown overalls and a greasy flat cap. His face and hands were streaked with oil.

'This way!' he said. 'Keep coming, you'll be all right.'

Dido walked up to him and said, 'Excuse me, who are you?'

The little man squinted at her.

'I could ask you the same question,' he said. 'You don't look like you come from round these parts.'

'I don't. I'm a visitor.'

The little man seemed pleased.

'A visitor, eh?' he chuckled. 'Can't say as we have many of them. And since you're so interested in who I am, young lady, I'll tell you. I'm the gatekeeper. I oil the hinges and keep the locks in good repair. When it's required, I open the gate and let people in, and when it's not required, I'm the one who closes the gate.'

'A-a-h, I get it!' said Dido. 'You're the switch, and these people are electrons in the current.'

The little man tutted.

'I know nowt about elect-er-ons,' he said. 'I just get on with me job.'

In her politest voice, Dido said, 'Would you mind showing me how you shut the gate?'

'Not at all,' said the little man. 'I go both ways, me. Open, shut – it's all the same as far as I'm concerned.'

He put his hand on the handle of the gate, pulled, and the gate closed with a loud clang.

Dido blinked – and she was back on the sofa in the lounge. The lamp was off and Dad was smiling at her.

'Well done, Dido,' he said. 'That was excellent. Now do it again.'

And Dido did it again – and again, and again, and again.

That evening, while Dad tried out a preview copy of a new computer game on his laptop and Mum tackled a stack of marking, Dido watched TV, dipping into soaps and sitcoms. This was partly relaxation and mostly research. TV programmes were a popular topic of conversation at school, and anyone who wasn't up to speed was classified as a weirdo. Dido, whose life was genuinely weird, liked to appear as normal as possible.

By nine o' clock, Dido could barely keep her eyes open. Waves of drowsiness coursed through her, sending her off into micro sleeps that made her lose track of what she was watching.

She zapped off the TV and stood up, stifling a yawn.

'I've had it,' she told her parents. 'I'm off to bed.'

She kissed Mum and Dad good night and went upstairs, closely followed by Cosmo.

When Dad heard Dido's bedroom door close, he turned to Mum and said, 'I'm worried that I might have pushed her too hard this afternoon.'

'She'll bounce back,' said Mum. 'She always does.'

Dad hesitated for a moment, then said, 'I've been getting a funny sort of feeling these last few days. Is it just me, or is the Dark One getting stronger?'

'No. I've noticed it too. Things are getting ragged at school. The number of pupils in detention is going through the roof. Something's wrong.'

Dad shut the lid of his laptop.

'Is it the Darkening?' he said.

'It might be the beginning. We'll have to tell Dido about it soon. I can't say that I'm looking forward to it.'

'We knew we'd have to tell her eventually. It's why we moved to Stanstowe.'

'True,' Mum agreed with a sigh, 'but that's not going to make it any easier. A noble sacrifice always seems a lot more noble when it's made by someone else's daughter, doesn't it?'

In her dream, Dido was riding a dapple-grey winged horse across a night sky. The great dark wings whooped as they beat through the air. The sky was bright with stars, bright enough for Dido to see her shadow against the horse's gleaming back.

The dream was more than real: Dido could feel the horse's warmth, smell its rich sweet scent, taste the sparkle of the starlight on her tongue. She was inside her magic, and its wildness made her laugh out loud.

Though it was night in the sky, far below the sun shone on the canopy of a vast forest. Silver rivers threaded their way through the dense green, and in the distance stood a range of black mountains with white peaks.

The horse straightened its wings and began a slow circle, down and down towards a clearing in the trees. As she drew nearer, Dido recognised the outcrop of boulders and the clear pool that lay at the centre of her magic.

The landing was as soft as the fall of a snowflake. Dido slid from the horse's back and walked towards the pool, where someone was waiting for her.

'Hello, Lilil,' Dido said.

Lilil had ash-blonde hair and was dressed in grey breeches and a loose-sleeved grey top. He or she – Dido had never been certain – was Dido's witch spirit. Like all witch spirits, Lilil had been born and reborn many times, most recently as Dido.

'Am I really here, or am I still dreaming?' said Dido.

'One or the other, yes,' Lilil said.

Dido concentrated. Lilil had an awkward habit of only answering the right questions, and whether a question was right or not was something that Lilil decided.

'Did you want to talk to me?' said Dido.

'No, but we need to talk.'

'What about?'

'You – what else?'

Dido took an intuitive leap.

'Has it got anything to do with the distractor?' she said.

'No.'

Dido put the question more precisely. 'Has it got something to do with the distractor?'

'Yes.'

'Who bewitched me?'

'Who do you think bewitched you?'

'That's what I've been trying to work out,' said Dido. 'I figured that it must have been a Shadowmaster, but there isn't a Shadowmaster in Stanstowe right now.'

'Don't figure – know!' Lilil said sternly.

Dido considered the possibilities and said, 'Could the last Shadowmaster have put the spell on me?'

'Isn't that what Shadowmasters do?' Lilil snorted.

'How come I didn't notice it? It didn't make my thumbs itch or anything.'

'The spell was set to work at the time of the Darkening.'

Dido heard the capital letter in Lilil's voice and shivered.

'What's the Darkening?' she said.

'Now is the Darkening. The Dark One that Shadowmasters serve is asleep, but he has begun to dream. He has been searching for someone to turn into another Shadowmaster who will help him to make his dreams take shape in your world, and he has found one who may prove suitable.'

'Who?'

'That's for you to discover yourself,' Lilil said. 'It should be easier now that you have disposed of the distractor. You must thwart the dark force. His dreams must not become real or he will wake before the Time of the Stars.'

'The Time of the Stars,' Dido murmured. She remembered how, in Stanstowe Museum, the portrait of a man who'd been dead for almost a century had spoken to her and used the same phrase. 'What'll happen if he does?'

'Blood, famine, war, ruin,' said Lilil. 'Both

our worlds will be laid waste.'

Lilil's voice sounded faint. The night in the sky seeped into the clearing, swallowing the trees, the boulders and the pool.

'So,' said Dido. 'I'm not even thirteen yet, I'm a schoolkid and I have to save the world. Great – this is just great!'

And the dream ended.

13
Shadows

The runaround was actually Alison's car, a tinny little French machine with red and white paintwork that made it look like a toy. Unlike Dad's company car, it didn't have air-conditioning, a radio or a CD player, and the windows were fastened with metal clips. Philippa was embarrassed whenever she rode in it and sat silent, hoping Alison could hear the silence above the sewing-machine rattle of the engine.

Outside the car, the sun shone brightly, and the weather forecast had promised the warmest spring day so far. Alison had opened her window, but its clip didn't work properly and it flapped like a spaniel's ear, the gusting draught blowing Philippa's hair this way and that.

The car left the dual carriageway and crawled along a street that was studded with sleeping policemen and choked with parked cars. A level crossing marked the boundary of Stanstowe. Beyond was farmland: grazing horses and cattle; fields filled with green spears of sprouted grain.

Alison said, 'Would you like me to pull into a farm shop so you can buy flowers?'

'No,' said Philippa. 'Mum didn't believe in that kind of thing. She said you should give flowers to people while they're still alive, not after they're dead.'

'Sensible lady.'

At a mini-roundabout, Alison turned left on to a tree-lined avenue. Philippa remembered the avenue on the day of Mum's funeral, looking as flat and unreal as a painted backdrop on a stage set.

'What was she like?'

The question threw Philippa off balance. 'Who?'

'Your mother. You mention her quite often, but you don't really talk about her. Sometimes it helps to talk.'

'That's what the family counsellor told us. She said we ought to share our memories of Mum.'

But Philippa hadn't taken the family counsellor's advice. She wanted to keep her memories to herself, not share them.

'What do you remember about her?' Alison asked.

'How funny and kind she was. How she never

broke a promise. When I was six, she threw a surprise birthday party for me. She did these candle things, with bits of banana standing up inside pineapple rings. There were pieces of Brazil nut in the tops of the bananas, and they burned like candle flames. When I saw she'd done all that for me, I—'

Philippa couldn't think of a word, because none of it was true. Mum had been considerate at times, but there had been other times when she was snappy and irritable. Her voice could sting worse than a slap.

'So she was the perfect mother?' said Alison.

'I wouldn't know. She was the only mother I had. There wasn't anybody I could compare her with.'

'My mother wanted me to be a doll. You know – ribbons in my hair, pretty frocks, don't speak until you're spoken to, don't step in puddles because you'll get your shoes dirty? I wanted to be out playing football with my brothers.'

'Didn't you tell her?'

'Oh yes.' Alison's voice turned posh, as it did when she used the phone. 'Football isn't for little girls, dear, it's such a rough game! Why don't you play with your Barbie instead?'

Alison laughed, and Philippa couldn't stop herself from joining in. She cut the laugh short; she shouldn't be laughing, going where she was going.

Alison said, 'It's OK to be happy, Philippa. I'm sure your mother wouldn't mind.'

Philippa didn't want to let on that Alison had read her thoughts. She decided that now was the moment to use the secret weapon she'd brought along.

'I've got the digital camera,' she said. 'Would you mind taking a photograph of me next to Mum's memorial?'

'Of course not, if that's what you want,' Alison said, and the kindness in her voice left Philippa feeling wrong-footed.

The Garden of Remembrance was a wide lawn, planted with rose bushes. The memorial plaques were set on white pegs, sticking up like the arms of schoolchildren eager to answer a question. Mum's plaque was small and simple, no In Loving Memory, just her name, Elizabeth Jane Trevelyan.

Philippa stared down at it. Why was she standing there? She was using Mum to get one up on Alison. What would Mum have thought about that?

A sudden rush of memory put Philippa in the present and the past simultaneously.

One night, about a month before the accident,

Mum and Dad had argued. Philippa heard their muffled voices rising through her bedroom floor.

Mum had shouted, 'If it wasn't for the kids, I would have—'

Philippa cut out the rest of the sentence by wrapping a pillow around her head. She whispered, 'Make them stop, make them stop!' over and over, until the front door slammed and the house went quiet.

Afterwards, it had been awful. Mum and Dad silently continued the row, being coldly polite when they had to talk to each other. Philippa sensed that something had gone badly amiss between them, but no one would explain what.

And two days before Mum died, she'd entered Philippa's room when Philippa should have been asleep, and softly said, 'I'm sorry, Pip,' before slipping out.

What had she meant – what had she been sorry for?

Philippa had forgotten about it until now. She'd clung to the image of her mother as a wonderful, saintly person who'd never done anything wrong. But it wasn't true.

A rising tide of anger made tears spill from

Philippa's eyes. She was angry with Alison, Dad, Tom, herself, but mostly with Mum. Philippa's shoulders jerked as she sobbed.

Alison said, 'Philippa?' and put an arm around Philippa's shoulders. Philippa didn't shy away; she needed someone to hold her up.

'Why did she go out that night?' she groaned. 'Why didn't she come back? Why did she have an accident? Why didn't she drive more carefully? How could she do this to us?'

Alison didn't reply. She held Philippa and stroked her hair, waiting for Philippa to cry herself out.

When Philippa's tears subsided, she and Alison walked back to the car. As they were getting in, Philippa said, 'I won't bother about the photo, Alison. I don't really want one.'

'I already took some, while you were looking at your mother's plaque.'

Philippa felt that she owed Alison something, so she said, 'Mum wasn't always the perfect mother. She could be a right cow when she was in a mood.'

'I know. Your father says you're just like her.' Alison's hand flew to her mouth. 'I'm sorry, Philippa! I didn't mean—'

Philippa could easily have pretended to be more

offended than she was in order to pick a quarrel with Alison, but much to her surprise, Philippa found that she didn't want to.

'It's OK,' she said. 'Dad's right.'

Alison slotted her seat belt into place and said, 'Is this a truce, Philippa?'

Philippa shrugged. 'A ceasefire, maybe.'

Tom was full of Chessington. All through dinner he described the rides in such exhaustive detail that finally Philippa couldn't stand any more. She said, 'Tom, Alison took some pictures this morning. Let's go and download them on to the computer.'

'Why don't you do it yourself?' said Tom.

'Er, because I don't know how? Come on, you can show me.'

'But—'

'Dad and Alison haven't seen each other all day. Let's give them some space.'

'You what?' said Tom, looking shocked – but he didn't look half so shocked as Dad.

Apart from the cables and fiddly plugs, downloading the digital camera was straightforward. The pictures were interesting, because they showed Philippa from Alison's point of view: a fair-haired girl wearing black clothes, gazing down at a plaque in the Garden of Remembrance, her face as confused and lost as the face of a refugee returning to a pile of rubble that had once been a home.

Tom said, 'Wei-rd!'

'What is?'

'In this one, you've got two shadows.'

Tom was right. There was Philippa's real shadow, slightly to one side of her, lying partly on the lawn, partly on the gravel path. Behind her was a second shadow, the shadow of someone taller and thinner.

'Wei-rd!' Tom said again.

14
The Stone Cage

Late Sunday afternoon, as the sun was setting, Malkin told Alice that she wanted to be taken out. Alice didn't know that she'd been told, and thought it was her own idea. Most people would consider it eccentric to take a cat for a walk, but Alice had always valued eccentricity, and Malkin wasn't like other cats. Over the years, she and Alice had developed a rapport that verged on telepathy.

Alice carried Malkin downstairs to the residents-only car park outside the block of flats. Some cats hated cars, but not Malkin, she was perfectly happy to curl up on the passenger's seat.

Alice started the engine and said, 'Where shall we go, Malkin?'

The cat mewed.

'Yes!' said Alice. 'That'd be good.'

On the way through town, Alice noticed three

young lads skulking in the entrance to an alleyway, smoking cigarettes. She recognised them as ex-pupils of hers, members of Seven North – no, it would be Eight North now. She'd disciplined them for bad behaviour so often that their names came automatically – Jack Farmer, Ross Williams and David Miller, known to staff and pupils alike as the Terrible Trio. Alice slowed down, intending to stop and give the trio a lecture about the effects of smoking on health, but a sharp growl from Malkin made her carry on.

'You're absolutely right,' she said. 'What they do outside school is none of my business.'

Alice drove out of Stanstowe, taking the road that climbed up Stanstowe Hill. At the top of the hill, she pulled over on to a grass verge, got out of the car and opened the passenger door so that Malkin could jump down. Malkin trotted towards the circle of the Speaking Stones, tail held high above her back. Alice followed her, feet squelching on earth that was still saturated with the late winter rains.

The sunset was dramatically lurid. The sky was a deep crimson, banded with scuds of magenta clouds whose undersides glowed golden in the last of the light. In the gathering dark, the stones were black silhouettes.

Alice peered into the gloom.

'Malkin?' she called. 'Where have you got to?'

'She is quite safe,' someone said.

Alice turned, startled, and saw a man standing just behind her.

He was middle-aged, fifty-something, Alice guessed; a tall, long-faced man with a bulbous nose, the corners of his mouth hidden by a thick, drooping moustache. His costume was quaint, a three-piece charcoal grey suit and a wing-collared shirt. A gold chain dangled across his waistcoat.

Though she was certain that she'd never met the man before, Alice found him oddly familiar.

'I do beg your pardon,' the man said. 'It was not my intention to alarm you.'

'That's all right,' said Alice.

The man held out his hand towards Stanstowe.

'This spot affords a fine vista for those who care for townscapes,' he said. 'As for myself, I prefer the stones. But please, allow me to introduce myself. My name is Edwin Langley-Davis,' and he gave a little bow.

'Alice Morgan,' Alice said. 'Do you live locally, Edwin?'

'I did once, long ago. I come back for the stones. They draw me. I have made something of a study of them.'

'Really?' said Alice. 'They're from the time of the Druids, aren't they?'

Edwin laughed. 'A common misconception, Miss Morgan. Romantic, perhaps, but inaccurate. The rituals of the Druids are modern compared with the age of this circle.'

'I wonder why it was built originally?'

'To be a cage,' Edwin said gravely, 'a great stone cage.'

Alice felt peculiar. There was a dry whispering in her ears, like the sound of sand being sifted on to paper, and Edwin's eyes seemed to be a luminous shade of violet – but that was impossible, no one had violet eyes. The shadows must be playing tricks with her.

'And what was put inside the cage?' she asked.

'My dear Miss Morgan, it would be far from advisable to discuss such matters at this hour.'

'This hour?'

'At twilight, when it is neither day nor night – a threshold time. There are other threshold times, naturally. New Year's Eve, noon and midnight spring to mind. At these moments nothing is certain, and ancient powers are at their strongest.'

The whispering was so loud that Alice could hardly hear what Edwin was saying.

'Powers?' she mumbled.

'Powers so far beyond the grasp of human reasoning that they cannot be understood, only felt. To serve them is an honour and a privilege. Service holds unimaginable dangers, but also brings rich rewards. The world, so to speak, is your apple, and you may take a bite from it whenever you wish.'

Alice shook her head, but the whispering continued. She began to make out voices, chanting words that made no sense.

'Palecorum alneth la,
Saletarum detha na...

'What does it mean?' she whispered. 'What are the voices saying?'

'They are offering an invitation, Miss Morgan. Watch closely!'

Edwin's face collapsed in on itself. His clothes shrank and shrivelled. His body dwindled into a wraith of purple mist that streamed through the air and coiled itself around Alice.

Alice's teeth chattered. She wanted to move, but something held her rooted to the spot. The mist stung the back of her nose as she breathed in. Her eyes closed and—

...She was stretched out on the sofa in her flat. Malkin was seated in the centre of the carpet, lashing her tail and angrily demanding to be fed.

Alice rubbed her eyes, and the last fragments of a weird dream disappeared from her mind.

'Sorry, Malkin! I must have dropped off for a few minutes.'

Alice clambered to her feet and went into the kitchen. The soles of her trainers grated against the vinyl floor tiles. Alice looked down and saw that she'd left a trail of dried mud behind her.

'Mud?' she murmured. 'Where did that come from?'

She tried to remember if she'd been out, but Malkin's mewing distracted her.

'Yes,' she said, bending to scratch the top of the cat's head. 'Dinner is served!'

Malkin purred.

15
Alarms

On Monday morning, while a part of Dido went through the routine of getting ready for school, the rest of her focused on the task that lay ahead. It wasn't going to be easy. The last Shadowmaster had come looking for her, and she'd been able to track him down; this time Dido had no idea of the kind of Shadowmaster she would have to deal with, or where he or she might be. Lilil hadn't provided any hard information, more a set of hints and vague warnings – but then Lilil was Dido's witch spirit, and magic was seldom logical. All Dido could do was stay on her toes.

Dido was still turning things over at the bus stop. She was so deep in thought that she didn't notice Scott was showing her a card trick until he gave up halfway through.

'Do let me know if I'm boring you, won't you,

Dido?' he said, putting the pack of cards back in his pocket.

'Sorry,' said Dido. 'I've got a lot on my mind at the moment. Magic stuff.'

'Oh?' Scott waited for Dido to continue. When she didn't he said, 'Don't worry, we'll soon be at school, then you'll be able to talk to Ollie about it.'

Dido caught the tone of resentment in Scott's voice and said, 'What's that supposed to mean?'

'It means that you bend Ollie's ear all the time. Funny, when I didn't believe you were a witch, you used to tell me about it. Now I know you're a witch, you tell me zilch.'

'That's not true!'

'Maybe, but Ollie gets to hear it first. I'm just the court jester. Scott and his pathetic tricks are always good for a laugh.'

'Who's rattled your cage?'

'You have, Dido,' said Scott. 'You've been dead grumpy lately. It's like you're so wrapped up in yourself that no one else matters – except for Ollie, that is. You're all smiles when you're with him.'

It didn't take any magic for Dido to know that Scott was jealous, and that she'd better do something fast.

'I'm sorry, Scott,' she said. 'I don't deliberately leave you out, and there's a good reason why I've been grumpy.'

'Yeah, Philippa,' said Scott.

So Dido had to explain about the distractor, which meant explaining about the new Shadowmaster. Dido had been hoping to avoid this, she didn't want any of her friends to get too involved in case they got hurt.

By the time she'd finished, things felt as though they were more or less back to normal, which was a plus. Dido figured that, given her current situation, she needed all the positive energy that she could get.

Monday mornings began with a double lesson of Art. Eight North's Art teacher was Mr Murray, an extremely tall man who was a talented artist in his own right, but whose true talent lay in talking, in which he could have competed at international level. He began as soon as Eight North entered the room, and was usually still talking when they left at breaktime. Dido's private theory was that he never actually stopped, but went on chuntering away whether there were pupils present or not.

This Monday for no apparent reason, Mr Murray had worked himself into a lather over chairs. He put a chair up on his desk so that everybody could see it, and asked what it was.

Seizing the chance to prove that he was a lad, Jack Farmer called out, 'Er, a chair, sir?' and smirked at his mates Ross and Kevin.

'Very perceptive, Jack,' said Mr Murray. 'How did you recognise it?'

'It's got four legs,' Terry said.

'So has a pitbull terrier, but I wouldn't recommend that you try to sit on one.'

'It's got a flat bit for sitting on,' Jack rapped back.

Mr Murray had an answer ready instantly.

'So, if I put a round cushion on the seat, it wouldn't be a chair?' he said.

Other people joined in the discussion, and after a lengthy question-and-answer session, Mr Murray came to the point.

'Each of us has a mental picture of what a chair should look like,' he said, 'and we compare that picture with any piece of furniture that might be a chair. In today's lesson, I want you to draw the perfect chair that you have in your mind.'

Dido saw her chair at once: a wooden throne,

carved with dragons and moons; in the centre of the high back was a sun disc, haloed in flame. Unfortunately, putting the throne on paper was nowhere near as straightforward as visualising it, and before long Dido was reaching into her pencilcase for an eraser.

She hesitated. If she pretended that she'd forgotten her eraser, it would give her an excuse to borrow one from Philippa, who was seated across the aisle. Dido knew that if she could just make eye contact with Philippa, it would be the start of putting things right between them – especially if she chucked in a persuasion spell to make Philippa remember all the good times that they'd spent together.

Dido turned her head and whispered, 'Philippa?'

As if responding to a cue, the bells rang in the corridor outside, not the quick double burst that marked the end of the lesson, but the continuous, ear-numbing jangle of a fire alarm.

Mr Murray snapped into action.

'Leave your things where they are and vacate the building,' he said. 'Line up on the tennis courts and wait for your form tutor to take a register.'

Outside, long queues of pupils filed across the campus. Teachers chivvied them along, rounding up stragglers as efficiently as Border collies in a sheepdog trial.

Mum was at the entrance to the tennis courts, looking harassed. Dido stopped for a moment to talk to her.

'Mum, is this a practice drill?' Dido asked.

'No,' said Mum, 'but it's not an actual fire either, thank goodness. The alarm system is playing up. It's affected the phones too, so we can't contact the security firm that services it.'

'Have you used inseeing to trace the problem?'

'Of course not!' Mum said. 'You know I don't mix magic and school unless it's absolutely necessary.' Mum suddenly realised that she was being Mum, and switched over to being Mrs Nesbit, the Deputy Head. 'Join the rest of your class, please,' she said coldly, as though Dido were someone she didn't know.

As she crossed the tennis courts, Dido had a flash of inspiration. She'd solemnly promised her parents never to use her magical powers at school – inseeing a teacher was too much like nosing into their private affairs – but this was a bit of an emergency, and an alarm system wasn't a person. It seemed that the new skill Dad had taught her on Sunday afternoon was going to come in handy after all.

Dido insaw, ignoring the seething crowds of pupils and their excited chatter. She concentrated on the nearest bell, the one fixed to the outside wall of the Sports Hall.

The bell turned into a man's face. His mouth was opened wide and he was bawling, 'Fire! Fire! Everybody out, out, out! Danger of death! Do not take personal possessions with you! Leave immediately! Fire! Fire!'

'There's no fire,' Dido said calmly.

The face looked at her.

'Isn't there?' it said. 'I wouldn't know about that. I do as I'm told, and I was told to ring, so I rang.'

'Who told you?'

'The lady. The purple lady.'

Dido flinched. Purple was the colour of Shadow Magic. The Shadowmaster must be a female, which narrowed Dido's search down to approximately half the population of Stanstowe, and someone who had access to the school.

Interesting, Dido thought. But first things first.

'OK,' she said. 'The purple lady told you to ring, and I'm telling you to stop.'

The face's eyes widened.

'Stop?' it gasped. 'I can't stop just like that. I've got

rules to follow. It's more than my job's worth.'

'If you don't, I'll blow your fuses.'

'You wouldn't!'

'Wouldn't I?' said Dido.

The bells stopped, and everyone on the tennis courts heaved a sigh of relief into the welcome silence.

But the relief and silence were short-lived.

The wind picked up, rapidly blowing itself into a gale that raked across the tennis courts. Eddies gusted mischievously, overturning litter baskets and swirling their contents into the air. Pupils huddled together as sweet wrappers and empty crisp-packets lashed their faces.

Dido, still inseeing, pinpointed the source of the disturbance.

A Shadow spell floated overhead, an enormous dark serpent with glossy scales and a forked purple-black tongue that darted from its mouth, whipping the wind into a cyclone.

From deep inside her, Dido's Shadow Magic responded instantly. It formed a spell that was shaped like a fiery wheel, spinning so fast that the spokes appeared to be running backwards.

The rim of the wheel broke the serpent's

backbone, caught the triangular head and narrow tail-tip in its spokes and burned the scaly body into oily black smoke.

There was a choking smell of seared flesh. All around the tennis courts, people hacked and retched.

After a brief consultation with the senior teachers, the Head, Dr Parker, made an announcement, his deep voice echoing off the surrounding buildings.

'The false fire alarm and the strong smell of burning suggest that there may be a fault in the school's electrical supply. In view of the potential risk, I have no choice but to close the school until the fault has been traced and repaired. Those of you who wish to contact your parents to arrange transport, please assemble in the Main Hall. Those of you who are able to make your own way home, don't forget to collect your belongings from the classrooms before leaving. Notice of the school's reopening will appear in the local press, Radio Stanstowe and on the Prince Arthur website.'

There were a few cheers.

Scott grinned at Dido and said, 'Top result!'

'Hmm!' said Dido. She wasn't as pleased as Scott. Shadowmasters loved disruption, and the pettier it was the more they loved it, but this disruption had been reckless, as if the Shadowmaster had wanted a large audience to be aware of her presence.

Dido's thumbs itched. They were telling her something, and she looked around to see if she could find out what it was.

'Scott,' she said, 'd'you see Miss Morgan anywhere?'

'She's with her form, Seven West, isn't she?'

'She ought to be, but she's not,' said Dido. She had a sneaking suspicion that she knew why, and things started slotting together.

Miss Morgan, the Sleeper who was bewildered by an inner force that she didn't understand, was someone who was wide open to the influence of the curse and the evil that lay behind it. She was the prime candidate for the new Stanstowe Shadowmaster. On the other hand, Dido couldn't be sure. She'd suspected Miss Morgan of being a Shadowmaster before, and got it totally wrong.

Dido sent a silent plea to the Goddess.

I could use a little help sorting things out here, she thought. Oh yeah, and by the way, why d'you always have to make things so complicated?

16
The Carousel

Philippa was home by eleven thirty. The house was empty, which was a relief because she needed time to think. Things were becoming clearer to her, and unpleasantly so. For the last few months she'd behaved like a total brat – moody with her family and friends, jealous of Dad and Alison's happiness, making life awkward in general for everybody. The person who'd come off worst was her. She'd isolated herself. The only person she confided in was thousands of miles away, and she only communicated with her via e-mail, which became more sad the more she thought about it.

Philippa had been hiding from the truth, punishing herself for something that was buried so deep that she couldn't dig down to it. She had a weird idea that it was connected with Mum's accident – but how?

She pushed the question aside and began to climb the stairs, intending to get changed out of her school uniform, but a sound made her stop halfway up. The fax machine on the telephone table in the hall buzzed and stuttered, even though the phone hadn't rung. Philippa watched the print-out rear against the paper support, like a cobra rising from a snake-charmer's basket. After the final long beep, she descended the stairs to read the message.

At first glance, the fax appeared to be hand-written, but when Philippa looked more closely, she saw that it was printed in a font that imitated handwriting.

How come you're not on-line, Storme?

That was all: no heading, no signature, no transmission details, but Philippa knew at once who'd sent it. She smiled, but the smile froze into a grimace as a frightening thought occurred to her. Zinny had somehow found out the fax number, and had known that Philippa would be there to receive it. Philippa shuddered, ducked into the lounge and switched on the computer.

So there you are!! Thought you must've given up on me.

Philippa frowned.

Zinny? How did you know I was in?

I have my methods. I heard your school got closed. Word gets around, you know?

Didn't you tell me that news travels slowly where you are?

Sometimes it does.

And I thought you lived far away from Stanstowe.

Sure I do, but I'm also closer than you think. I told you it was hard to explain. Did you like the picture?

What picture?

The one Alison took yesterday. Notice my shadow next to yours?

Philippa frowned harder.

It couldn't have been your shadow, Zinny, you weren't even there.

I kind of was. Ask Tom to tell you about image manipulation. You can get some neat effects.

You changed the photograph?

Uh-huh.

You can't have! Tom downloaded it and we looked at it straightaway. You didn't have time to change it.

Wrong!!! I work fast, Storme!! Things are easier with

Alison, right?

Philippa started. Either Zinny was incredibly intuitive, or something very creepy was going on.

How did you know?

No big deal. I figure you don't let somebody you don't like take your picture while you're standing at your mom's grave - or memorial, or whatever.

How d'you know it was Mum's memorial?

Well, duh!! Who else would you go visit in a Garden of Remembrance, Storme? It doesn't take rocket science to work that one out!!

The answer was a just little too slick, but Zinny didn't give Philippa long to wonder about it.

What did Alison do to make you change your mind?

I haven't. Not completely anyway.

But you don't want to cut her in two with a chainsaw any more?

It wasn't anything Alison did. It was Mum – and me.

Whoa, run that past me again! Your mom did something that made you change your mind about Alison?!

I haven't been remembering her properly.

Who - Alison?

No, Mum. She wasn't perfect. I shut out the bad times, pretended that there hadn't been any.

Gotcha! Doing a little image manipulation with her

memory so she came out better than she actually was?

Something like that.

The old never-speak-ill-of-the-dead trip, huh? That doesn't do dead people any favours, you know? They'd rather be remembered for real.

You're an expert on what dead people want? Is there anything you don't know, Zinny?

Yeah. I don't know the way out of here.

Out of where?

I'm not sure I know the answer to that, but wherever it is, it's the *pits*, Storme!! You have no idea.

What's keeping you there?

Me. Know when you've got a scab on your knee or something, and you keep picking at it, even though it hurts and you know you're making it worse? It's kind of like that - gross but fascinating.

What is?

Being here is.

Zinny, what country are you in?

That is one B-I-G question, Storme!

The front door opened. Philippa turned her head and saw Dad in the doorway of the lounge, looking astonished.

'Philippa?' Dad said.

'School's closed,' Philippa explained. 'There's

some problem with the electricity, so Dr Palmer sent everybody home.'

Dad nodded and said, 'What are you doing?'

'Chatting to a friend over the Internet.'

'Don't you think you should get on-line first?' Dad asked in his tactful voice.

Philippa laughed, 'I am on—'

But she wasn't. All the Internet tools had gone from the menu bar, leaving a plain grey screen.

'I was, er, just about to go on-line,' Philippa said quickly.

'Is something wrong with the fax?'

'Not as far as I know – why?'

'Because it's spat out a page with nothing on it. Maybe school isn't the only place with electrical problems.' Dad glanced at his watch. 'I'd better get my skates on and grab a bite. I'm meeting Alison at Tom's school – swimming gala. That's why I'm home early. Can I get you something?'

'Not just yet,' Philippa said.

Dad disappeared into the kitchen. Philippa sneaked into the hall to check the fax.

The message from Zinny had vanished.

Philippa's pulse pounded in her temples and she took some deep breaths to try and calm her mounting panic. It didn't make sense. What kind of girl could get into a computer, play about with downloaded photographs, take the machine off-line and send faxes that unprinted themselves? Philippa wasn't that up on technology, but she suspected that what Zinny had done wasn't possible.

She followed Dad into the kitchen. He was preparing a toastie, buttering pieces of bread on both sides. A pack of cheese slices lay open on the work surface.

'Dad,' said Philippa, 'if you were using a programme on the computer, could someone else on another computer shut the programme down?'

'Only by using magic,' Dad said sarcastically.

Philippa fell silent.

Dad popped his sandwich into the toastie maker and said, 'Why don't you come to the swimming gala, seeing as you're not at school?'

'I want to go and see a friend of mine this afternoon. I need her advice about something.'

'Oh – what?'

'Girls' stuff,' said Philippa, and went to call Dido.

*

Zinny was riding on a carousel, astride a wooden horse. The other horses had no riders. Their teeth were bared and their lilac-rimmed eyes protruded madly. A steam organ played a wheezy waltz with some notes missing, so that the melody was skewed.

The man was on the carousel, dressed as an old-time fairground attendant, in shirtsleeves, a brocade waistcoat and a curly-brimmed bowler hat made from purple felt. He made his way over to Zinny, steadying himself on the metal poles that held the horses in place.

'Enjoying yourself?' he said.

'No,' said Zinny. 'This carousel is me. I go round and round, and never get anywhere.'

'But it is still preferable to how things were before we met, is it not?'

'I'm not sure,' Zinny said. 'Before, it was mine. I could take a break when I wanted. It was kind of peaceful, you know? I never get to sleep here, no matter how tired I get. Sometimes I miss the old place a lot.'

The man raised an eyebrow far enough for it to disappear under the brim of his hat.

'What do you miss?' he said.

'The stillness. The quiet. The dark.'

'They could be yours again – but be warned. There will be no turning back. Once you return, you return for all eternity.'

'I wouldn't mind.' Zinny looked up into the blank,

violet haze of the sky. 'This place makes me antsy.'

The man scowled.

'Then your usefulness is drawing to an end,' he said. 'I shall release you soon.'

'How soon is soon?'

'That is for me to decide.'

The man waved his left hand. The carousel and the halting waltz accelerated. All Zinny could see was a blur. She seized the pole in front of her with both hands and squeezed until her knuckles showed white.

17
Presences

Dido and Philippa met on neutral ground – the Langley-Davis Park, which was just behind the Town Hall. The park's main feature was an enormous stone lion snarling on a plinth, a memorial to some forgotten Victorian war. Beside the statue stood a bandstand, though as far as Dido knew no bands ever played there.

Spring had well and truly arrived in the flowerbeds, and staff from nearby offices were eating lunch on the lawns and benches, taking advantage of the sunshine.

Dido and Philippa walked slowly along the path that ran past an ornamental fountain, then dipped down below the archway of a small bridge. Past the bridge lay the ruins of Stanstowe Abbey, crumbling flint-studded walls that looked like decaying molars.

Things didn't go well at first. Both girls were aware

that their friendship needed to be rescued, and neither was certain how, so their conversation was patched with awkward silences, but in the cool shadows of the ruined abbey Philippa opened out.

'I'm sorry, Dido,' she said.

'For?'

'For being...well, like I've been.'

'I'm sorry too,' Dido admitted. 'I haven't given you much sympathetic support, have I?'

'I don't blame you. I've been a right cow.'

'Likewise,' said Dido. 'Shall we form a herd?'

They both laughed and cut the laugh short because it sounded strangely muffled by the ancient masonry.

'So,' Dido went on, 'what's so important that you didn't want to talk about it over the phone?'

'Zinny.'

'Ah, your Net buddy.'

Philippa was surprised.

'You know about her?' she said.

'Ollie mentioned her. He's worried that she's having a bad influence on you.'

'So am I!' Philippa said, and she told Dido all about Zinny: Storme, the e-mails, the photograph, the mysterious fax, the shut down programme.

When Philippa was done, Dido said, 'Spooky, but you're talking to the wrong person. You'd be better off with my dad, he's the computer buff.'

'I don't need a computer buff, I need you.'

'Why me?'

Philippa lowered her voice and said, 'Because I think Zinny's using magic, and you're a witch.'

Dido stared in astonishment. 'You mean you know?'

'Of course I know. Remember that weird Drama lesson last year, when I floated off the floor? You saved me with magic, didn't you?'

'But you didn't say anything about it!' Dido spluttered. 'I haven't said anything till now because I wasn't sure if you could handle it. I've been walking on eggshells around you for the past twelve months.'

'What was I supposed to say?' Philippa wailed. 'It's not every day you find out that your best mate is a witch. Dabbling with Black Magic isn't your average kind of hobby, is it? You can't just drop it into a casual chat – "Oh hi, Dido. How's the cauldron?"'

'I don't have a cauldron and I don't dabble with Black Magic,' Dido growled. 'Black Magic is for weirdos. I'm a Light Witch.'

'What's the difference?'

'My magic works.'

'I'll take your word for it,' Philippa said. 'I never mentioned about you being a witch because it was nothing to do with me. That's not why I wanted to be friends with you.'

'Then why did you want to be friends?'

Philippa heaved an exasperated sigh.

'Because I *liked* you!' she snapped. 'You're fun, and a laugh, and I trust you, OK?'

The contrast between what Philippa was saying and the angry way in which she was saying it suddenly struck both girls as funny, and they dissolved into giggles. This time they didn't stifle their laughter, abbey or no abbey, and it brought them back together.

Philippa wiped tears from her eyes with a scrappy tissue.

'Can you help me, Dido?' she asked.

'It all depends.' Cautiously, Dido said, 'D'you mind if I insee you?'

'Do I mind if you *what*?'

'Inseeing's a bit like mindreading, but it works on feelings, not thoughts. Magic leaves a trace. If someone's put a spell on you, I should spot something.'

'What do I have to do?'

'Nothing. Concentrate on Zinny and I'll take care of the rest.'

Philippa gave Dido a wary glance. 'Will it hurt? You won't do anything yukky, will you?'

'Relax, Philippa. There's no newts' eyes or bats' claws involved, I promise. Just stay quiet a minute, all right?'

Inseeing transformed the abbey. Each patch of moss and lichen on the stones gave off an aura-light, glowing red, or yellow, or green, like soft gems. Memories seeped from the walls. Dido heard a choir singing, smelled incense and candlesmoke, felt damp air on her skin. The abbey was eager to tell her its story, but she ignored it and focused on Philippa.

Philippa's aura was pale blue, and rippled. Dido used a spell made from magnifying glasses and video cameras, and zoomed in closer.

Something was there, the hint of an echo flickering between the ripples. Dido sensed a presence and a yearning hunger.

'Who are you?' she said gently.

The echo instantly flitted away, faster than a startled cat.

And Dido understood who and what Zinny was.

She came out of her trance, blinking at a world that seemed flatter and duller than what she'd just seen.

'Was that it?' demanded Philippa.

'Pretty much.'

'I thought it would be more spectacular.'

'Sorry to disappoint you. All the special effects happen on the inside.'

'Did you find anything?'

Dido smacked her lips.

'Can we grab a juice somewhere?' she said. 'I'm parched.'

Philippa placed her hands on her hips. 'You *cannot* do that, Dido! If something weird's going on, I want to know about it.'

'And I'll tell you,' said Dido, 'but not here. It's too much like a horror-movie set. When I give you *this* information, you'll be glad to have people around you.'

Though they were unaware of it, while Dido and Philippa were talking in the abbey ruins, Alice Morgan was nearby, in the Town Hall Museum. She was standing in front of a full-length portrait of the man she'd met on Stanstowe Hill, Edwin Langley-Davis. Only according to the title on the frame he was Edwin Langley-Davis, first Lord

Stanstowe (1844-1921) – yet she was talking to him. Alice wasn't quite certain how this could be happening, but it didn't seem peculiar. She was in a state where talking without using words to a painting of a man long in his grave seemed perfectly natural.

'Good day, Alice,' said the portrait. 'I hope you will allow me to call you Alice?'

'Please do, Edwin.'

The painted mouth broke into a smile. 'A little bird tells me that you used your power today. How did that feel?'

Alice struggled to find an adequate word.

'Wonderful!' she said. 'I didn't know that anything could feel so wonderful.'

'You also had the satisfaction of inconveniencing those who have inconvenienced you,' said Edwin. 'The students and colleagues who take your talents for granted when they have no concept of how great those talents are.' The expression on Edwin's face changed from kind to serious. 'However, Alice my dear, you must exercise considerable caution.'

'Must I?'

'This morning's prank, though undoubtedly delicious, may prove to have been a trifle ill-advised. It has alerted an enemy to your presence.'

Alice felt a pang of anxiety, and for a moment the sheer ludicrousness of holding an imaginary conversation with an oil-painted canvas made her doubt her sanity. Then she saw the strangely coloured light in Edwin's eyes that she'd noticed at their last meeting, and her doubts faded away. The light was so soothing and reassuring that she could have looked at it for hours on end.

'I have enemies?' she said.

'Formidable enemies,' said Edwin. 'But if you listen carefully to me, you will have the measure of them. When I have finished speaking, go home and wait for me to contact you.'

Edwin spoke rapidly in a language that Alice hadn't heard before, but seemed to be able to understand.

The portrait stilled into pigment; the audience was finished.

Alice turned, and saw that a male museum attendant was smiling at her from his chair across the way.

'Getting to know old Edwin then?' he enquired cheerfully.

'Edwin?' said Alice. 'Oh, the painting! It's very striking isn't it?'

The attendant nodded.

'Some mornings when I open up, I'd swear he was about to come to life and step out in to the room,' he said. 'His eyes follow you everywhere, you know. No matter where you stand, old Edwin's watching you.'

'I'm sure he is,' said Alice.

Dido and Philippa went to the Regency, a coffee bar in the George Arcade. Most of the shops in the arcade were boarded up, but the Regency managed to stay in business, even though it didn't appear to have been redecorated since the Seventies. The counter was dominated by a large and aged espresso machine, and there wasn't a sun-dried tomato or kiwifruit in sight. The Regency was strictly a cheese-and-pickle sandwich and sticky bun sort of place.

The old-fashioned decor and low prices had made the cafe borderline trendy, and Dido recognised a few Prince Arthur pupils among the customers. She treated Philippa to a Diet Coke, bought herself a watery orange juice and they went to sit at a table in one corner.

Philippa was twitchy, and spilled some of her drink.

'I'm nervous, Dido,' she confessed.

'Don't be,' said Dido. 'If I'm right about Zinny, she couldn't do anything to hurt you if she wanted to, and I don't think she does.'

'Then what does she want?'

'Company. She's lonely – *really* lonely. You're the first person she's been in touch with for a long while.'

'But she's talked to me about her parents, and she must have friends at school, mustn't she?'

'I don't think so.'

'What's her problem?'

Dido hesitated. She didn't know quite how to tell Philippa what she'd found out about Zinny, but she was going to have to. She took a deep breath. 'She's dead,' said Dido.

'Dead? How can she be dead when—' Realisation drained the colour from Philippa's face. 'Oh, my God, you mean Zinny's a ghost?'

'That's one way of putting it, but don't get her wrong,' said Dido. 'Zinny's not one of those evil, chain-rattling spooks that you get in horror movies. She's more like a tourist whose visa's expired.'

Dido had known it would be difficult for Philippa to grasp. She took a sip of juice and said, 'Not everyone who dies is ready for it. Death can be unexpected, and some people have difficulty in adjusting. They go into denial, hang on to all the things they knew in this world, and a part of them stays behind.'

'Their soul?' Philippa said.

Dido pulled a face. 'Not their soul exactly.'

'Then what?'

'You know when Dr Parker walks on stage in the Main Hall to take morning assembly?' said Dido. 'He doesn't do anything or say anything, but everybody goes quiet. His presence makes them do it. That's the part that stays behind.'

Philippa thought about this for a few seconds, then said, 'So I should really be feeling sorry for Zinny, not afraid of her.'

'Right. Zinny's incredibly mixed-up. She's between things – she's alive and she isn't, she's there and she's not. She knows that she has to move on, but she's scared of what it'll be like. We have to convince her that it's OK.'

'How?' Philippa said.

'We talk to her.'

Philippa shivered. 'What I don't get is, why me? Why did Zinny make contact with me of all people?'

'I haven't figured that out yet,' said Dido. 'Maybe we should get on-line and ask her.'

'When?'

'Now seems like a good time.'

Dido was nowhere near as confident as she sounded, and she hadn't been straight with Philippa. She strongly suspected that Philippa and Zinny had been deliberately set up, but by whom, and why?

Dido scratched her itching thumbs. She didn't know exactly what she was getting herself into, but all her witch instincts told her that Shadow Magic was involved somewhere, and where there was Shadow Magic, there was always a Shadowmaster.

18
Cleansing

Alice Morgan had never felt anything like it before. It was a whole new way of feeling, one that went beyond the reach of words. It wasn't fear or joy, exhilaration or grief, but a mixture of everything, a flood of sensation that carried her along. She had a dark flame inside her, a burning shadow that consumed the Alice Morgan she'd once been.

'I've been reborn!' she told Malkin.

Malkin, who was seated in the kitchen doorway, blinked slowly, thrashed her tail and mewed impatiently.

'Yes,' said Alice. 'I'll speak to him soon, let me just enjoy this a while longer.'

She had discovered that there were two worlds. The reality she'd taken for granted was only a thin membrane, stretched over a vaster, deeper reality. Even something as everyday as a stroll around the town centre had been a revelation. Another Stanstowe slept beneath the Stanstowe she knew. She'd almost been able to glimpse the outlines of the buildings that lay under the bricks and concrete.

The people on the streets had seemed half asleep, unaware of the wonders that surrounded them. Alice pitied them. They were no better than sheep or cattle, roaming aimlessly, and she would have to herd them: because the world below the world was going to be hers. She'd known it outside the Pentacle, when she'd stood in the centre of the bridge that crossed Holywell Brook and seen the stream for what it was – a flow of energy that could carve its way through stone, given enough time. The head of the stream was a spring on the side of Stanstowe Hill, a place where rocks wept. The water rose from the darkness of the earth into the light, a link between what was hidden and what was open for all to see.

But they didn't see. Their minds were too small. Only Alice saw, and she knew that her vision meant she'd been singled out. She was privileged; special.

A shadow in a corner of the room hardened and grew into Edwin, looking exactly the same as in his portrait. Alice wasn't alarmed. She'd been expecting him.

'You are quite right,' Edwin said. 'You are special, my dear Alice. Very special indeed. You have been chosen to prepare the way. You will bring the Darkening to its finest flowering.'

'The Darkening?' said Alice.

'The Darkening is a time of cleansing, when all obstacles must be removed from his path. The time of the stars approaches, and you must make ready for when he wakes.'

'Who are you talking about?' Alice asked, bewildered.

The weird light shone in Edwin's eyes.

'The Dark One,' he said. 'My spirit is his mouthpiece. What you have now has been granted to you by him. He has lent you a little of his strength. The use you make of it will be a test of your worthiness.'

'How can I prove I'm worthy?'

Edwin's tone became harsh.

'Your enemies and the Dark One's enemies are one and the same,' he said. 'Root them out and destroy them. Leave no trace of them behind to sully the Darkening.'

'I'll see to it straightaway,' Alice said with her sweetest smile. 'Come, Malkin!'

Edwin shook his head. 'This is something you have to do alone. Malkin will be safer here with me.'

Alice's pang of disappointment didn't show in her voice as she said, 'Yes, Edwin. Just as you say.'

The drive across town was ultra-smooth and hassle free. All the traffic lights were on green and every time Alice needed to change lanes, an obliging motorist let her pull over. Normally, Alice would have put it down to coincidence, but nothing was normal today, and there was no such thing as coincidence. The power within her was at work.

Alice relaxed at the wheel and searched her memories. Her whole life had been leading up to this moment, she realised, although she hadn't realised while she'd been living it. She'd always had power, like her mother. 'The Way,' Mum had called it. Mum had always been fiddling with herbs and potions, brewing up concoctions that tasted vile and smelled worse. Alice had stubbornly resisted all her mother's attempts to teach her the Way. As far as Alice was concerned it was just superstitious nonsense, and she'd have nothing to do with it. She'd been the first member of her family to stay on into the sixth form, and to go to university, and she'd firmly believed that education was all the power she needed. That belief was wrong, and Alice had paid the price. For years she'd been in denial about her magic, suppressing it instead of exploring it, but those days were over. Surrender had liberated her.

Alice turned off Stanstowe Road, into one of the newish estates, and cruised past rows of identical houses. She didn't know exactly where she was going – the car seemed to be driving itself – but she recognised the place as soon as she got there. There was no mistaking it.

Alice's magic showed her that the house was well protected. The spells surrounding it arced and bowed like an animated diagram of a magnet's lines of force, shimmering in rainbow colours that reminded Alice of oilstains on wet tarmac. For a few minutes she watched the spells moving, fascinated by their beauty, then she lowered her eyes. The car in the driveway was familiar. Alice had seen it hundreds of times in school, parked in the space reserved for the Deputy Head, Mrs Nesbit.

A flash of the old Alice returned. Faye Nesbit had been supportive, sympathetic, more like a friend than a senior member of staff. She'd done nothing to harm Alice, far from it, and she didn't deserve what was about to happen to her.

This whole situation is crazy! Alice thought.

Her magic surged and her thoughts changed. The house was loathsome, the lair of the enemy. Alice stopped the car and got out. She knew what had to be done.

19
Lost and Found

Dido and Philippa caught a bus at one of the stops outside Stanstowe Station. Dido felt apprehensive about what she was about to face, and that wasn't good. If she had to deal with Shadow Magic, she needed to be flexible and spontaneous. Thinking about it too much in advance might prove to be a handicap. So, in order to get her mind working on something else, she said, 'How are things at home?' even though there was a risk that she'd have to sit through yet another session of Philippa's grumbling.

'Not so bad,' Philippa said.

Dido was surprised. 'Really?'

'Alison and I aren't best buddies or anything, but we understand each other a bit better.'

'When did this happen?'

Philippa shivered.

'That's why it's so freaky about Zinny,' she said. 'She gave me a lot of advice. Her e-mails made me take a new look at things.'

'Such as?'

Philippa glanced out of the bus window to buy herself some time. What she was going to admit to Dido wasn't easy, because she was also admitting it to herself.

'My mum,' she said. 'I've been fooling myself about her, only remembering the stuff I wanted to remember. She wasn't as perfect as I've been making out. She married Dad because...' Philippa blushed. 'I was born six months after the wedding. They had to get married because of me.'

Philippa sounded so miserable that Dido said, 'But that wasn't your fault. Don't blame yourself.'

'Mum used to blame me. Sometimes, when she lost her temper, she'd tell me that if it hadn't been for me, she'd be somewhere else, having a different life.'

Before she could stop herself, Dido burst out, 'The cow!' then quickly added, 'I'm sorry. I—'

'It's OK,' said Philippa. 'You're right. My mother wasn't perfect.'

'Is that what Zinny told you?'

'No, but she got me to the point where I could say it.'

Dido was puzzled. It didn't sound much like Shadow Magic to her. Shadow Magic didn't go around sorting out people's problems, it messed with their heads and turned them into wrecks. The story of Snow White and the Seven Dwarves was a perfect example. The Wicked Queen hadn't started off wicked, but she'd somehow got hold of a magic mirror – a Shadow Magic mirror to be precise – and it had twisted her until she was insanely jealous of her stepdaughter.

But Shadow Magic seemed to have helped Philippa to make an emotional breakthrough.

Something was wrong here, and Dido wished that she knew what it was.

Dido hadn't been to Philippa's house for several weeks, and the first thing she noticed was the different atmosphere. During her last visit, the house had felt awkward and prickly. Now it was warm and friendly, more at ease with itself. Not the lounge though – or more specifically, not the computer in the lounge. It gave off the smell of old Shadow Magic, a sour rotten smell, like curdled milk and mouldy vegetables.

Philippa moved towards the chair in front of the computer.

'Stay where you are,' said Dido. 'Don't get too close to the computer.'

'How can I turn it on without getting close to it?' Philippa asked, reasonably enough.

'I'll take care of it. I can turn it on from here.'

'How?'

'With magic.'

Dido tuned in to herself and waited until the rhythm of her heartbeat told her that she was ready. She fixed her inseeing on the dark dead screen of the monitor, and her magic drew her inside.

She was in a thick fog, visibility down to no more than two metres. A choking dampness filled her lungs and made her cough. Straight ahead was a faint light, blurred to a stain. Dido made for it, hoping she wouldn't trip over anything.

As she got closer, Dido saw that the light was a neon sign – Startup Club & Bar. Below the sign was a doorway, and in front of the doorway was a man. He was tall, with such broad shoulders that Dido wondered if he'd forgotten to take the hanger out of his dinner jacket. He wore a stiff-fronted white shirt, a black bowtie and wraparound mirror shades.

It didn't take long for Dido to put it together – Startup was the big clue. The man in the DJ had to be the computer's equivalent of the gatekeeper she'd met in the table lamp. She approached him with what she hoped was a winning smile.

'Hi!' she said. 'Terrible weather, isn't it?'

'What you want?' the man grunted.

'You're the switch, right?'

The man scowled.

'I'm a nightclub security operative,' he said.

'Excuse me?'

'A bouncer. I let people in, and I sort 'em out if they make trouble.'

Guessing that a little flattery wouldn't go amiss, Dido said, 'Gosh, that sounds like an important job.'

The man straightened his jacket and ran a hand over his close-cropped hair.

'You're not wrong there,' he said. 'Not much goes on here until I give the say so.'

'I don't suppose you'd open up for me, would you?'

'No chance, sweetheart. These are licensed premises, and you're well underage.'

'Oh, go on!' Dido wheedled. 'I only want a peep. I've never seen the inside of a club before. I promise I won't touch anything. Pl-e-e-a-se?'

The man sucked air in through his teeth, pulled his bottom lip and sighed.

'All right then, but make it quick,' he said.

He touched the handle of the door, and everything changed.

A city sprang up all around Dido. Skyscrapers towered up into the purple glare of the sky, their plate glass windows reflecting the lights of the signs that were everywhere – Abe's Diner, The Golden Gulch Casino, 1st Avenue Bank, Wendell's Repository. The signs stretched down the long, wide street for as far as Dido could see. Bright flashes zipped along the road, faster than the tracks of shooting stars. The whole city was bustling energetically.

Dido set off along the broad pavement and stopped when she realised that something was missing.

Where are the people? she thought.

A notice in the window of Abe's Diner said, EAT. The glass and chrome fittings gleamed invitingly, but all the tables and chairs were empty and the counter was untended. It was the same wherever Dido looked. The shops, bars and hotels were lit up as though they were open for business, but there didn't seem to be any takers.

The further Dido went into the city, the more her

impression of it changed. At first she'd been impressed by its glamour, but she gradually became aware that it was hollow at its centre, and as the sense of hollowness grew, her surroundings altered. Broken panes appeared in the high-rises' windows. Dido passed boarded-up doors, the boards sprayed with swearwords. In places walls had crumbled, spilling broken bricks on to the pavement. The paving stones turned grimy, blotched with black polka dots of hardened chewing gum.

The neon faded. The skyscrapers shrank into dilapidated three-storeyed buildings from an earlier century. Alleyways ran between them, gaping like yawning mouths. Dido stopped, uncertain whether she should carry on or go back, and looked around.

A hand-painted sign was fixed to the wall of a nearby building, illuminated by a row of light bulbs with gaps in it – Lost and Found. A peeling red arrow pointed downwards to an open door.

Lost and Found? thought Dido. That'd be right.

She went inside. A narrow passageway led to another open door, where a light shone. Dido followed the passageway, her trainers sticking to the rotting linoleum that covered the floor, and entered a cramped room. Inside was a bare wooden table, lit by an oil lamp. Seated behind the table was a girl, the top half of her face in shadow, arms folded across her chest. When the girl opened her mouth to speak, lamplight glinted on the braces that covered her teeth.

'That you, Storme?' she said.

'No, I'm Dido. Storme couldn't come. You must be Zinny.'

'I guess I must be too. Did the guy send you?'

Dido frowned.

'What guy?' she said.

'The creepy guy with the purple smile.'

Does she mean the Shadowmaster? thought Dido. All her mental alarms went off at once, but she kept her voice even.

'No one sent me,' she said. 'Coming here was my idea. We need to talk.'

Zinny obviously needed to talk, because words suddenly poured out of her.

'He is such a fink!' she said. 'You ought to have heard the promises he made me! He was going to do this, he was going to do that. I was going to be the belle of the ball, prom queen and president rolled into one, and all I had to do was talk to Storme. Only, what did I get? Diddly squat! He ran out on me, didn't even tell me the way out. If I ever see him again, I'm going to—'

'Why did he want you to talk to Storme?' Dido interrupted.

Zinny unfolded her arms and turned up her palms.

'Beats me,' she said. 'He told me a bunch of stuff, but I didn't listen to half of it. Boy, could he ever talk once he got going.'

There was no time for Dido to be tactful, it was now or never.

'Zinny,' she said, 'you know that you shouldn't be here, don't you?'

Zinny's mouth grinned.

'Sorry,' she said, 'but I just love your accent. It's kind of cute.'

'You know you shouldn't be here,' said Dido.

The edges of Zinny's grin pulled down.

'I know,' she said. 'I want to rest, but how do I do it? The guy said he was going to get me out of here.'

'His kind never keeps promises.'

'Yeah, tell me about it.'

Dido softly sang a lullaby. It had originally been intended to soothe tetchy babies, but Dido had added a few variations to it.

Zinny put her head on one side to listen.

'Sleep now, gentle, sleep now low,
Dawn will come before you know.
Rest your head and close your eyes,
And wait for morning's sun to rise.'

Zinny let out a long breath and said, 'Will it be like that, sort of comfy and cosy?'

'I think so.'

'Will my family be there?'

'I don't know,' Dido said honestly.

'But anywhere has to be better than here, huh?'

The notes of the lullaby were beginning to take effect. The wall behind Zinny grew as thin as gauze. Beyond it was a thickly starred night sky. A gust of wind whisked the last of the wall away. Zinny felt the draught on the back of her neck, and turned her head.

'Wow, it's beautiful!' she gasped. 'I didn't think it would be so beautiful. Can I really go there? You're not lying, are you?'

'I wouldn't lie,' said Dido.

The starry sky was drifting into the room, billowing like cloud.

'What do I have to do?' Zinny said.

'Let go.'

Zinny nodded. 'Yeah, I could do that. That would

be neat. Thanks, Dido. Been nice talking to you.'

'And you,' Dido said.

The stars went out. Shapes formed in the darkness – furniture, bookshelves, Philippa. The shapes brightened until they were real.

'Zinny's gone,' Dido said.

'Already?' said Philippa. 'But you only just—'

'Time isn't the same in magic.'

'You're sure she's gone?'

'Positive.'

Philippa's shoulders slumped.

'I'm going to miss her,' she said.

Philippa shed a few tears. When they were over, Dido told her about the city and the Lost and Found. When she came to the part about the starry sky, Philippa broke in and said, 'That's lovely! Is it like that for everybody?'

Dido shrugged. 'Who knows? Zinny made the city out of her memories, and it was a bad place for her to be. The lullaby spell helped her to find the right place.'

'Huh?' said Philippa.

While Dido was trying to explain, her mobile phone rang.

It was Mum.

'Dido? I want you to come home.'

'Why – what's up?'

'Nothing,' Mum said. 'Your father and I have got a surprise for you.'

Mum sounded bright – far too bright.

'What kind of surprise?' Dido asked suspiciously.

'One that can't wait. You'll find out when you get home. Don't be long.'

'I won't be.'

Dido was just about to press the Cancel button, when she heard something in the background on the other end of the line that made the hairs on the nape of her neck stand up.

Cosmo was howling, and even if she hadn't been able to understand Cat, Dido would have recognised the yowl as a shout for help.

20
In the Dark Ravine

Time slowed down.

Dido phoned for a taxi, and the five-minute wait before it picked her up at Philippa's house seemed more like an hour. Philippa sensed that something was wrong, asked Dido what and wasn't convinced by Dido's denials. When the taxi arrived, Dido had to practically slam the door in Philippa's face to prevent her from tagging along. Dido felt guilty, but figured that she had enough on her plate already, without adding worrying about Philippa to it.

The taxi became snarled in heavy traffic, and no amount of willing on Dido's part could accelerate its progress to more than a crawl. Nor did telling herself to stay calm do much to quell the mounting fear that chewed at her insides like the jaws of a big cat.

Now, when it was too late, she realised how tightly she'd been snared. The dark power that Lilil had spoken of had been busy. It had used the distractor to keep Dido focused on Philippa, and manipulated Philippa and Dido to make Dido think that Philippa was at risk. All the time, the danger had been where Dido least expected it – in her own home. The thought of what might be happening to Mum, Dad and Cosmo made her feel sick.

Dido told the taxi driver to drop her on the corner of Mistletoe Lane, walked cautiously towards the house, and noticed that Miss Morgan's car was parked at the side of the road. Dido's first hunch about the identity of the new Shadowmaster had been right after all.

Next time you have a hunch like that, Dido said to herself, *do* something about it!

At least she knew who, if not what, was waiting for her, and Dido tried to be optimistic. She guessed that Miss Morgan had been possessed by Shadow Magic, and that the possession was recent. Miss Morgan couldn't have had much experience, and that might just give Dido an edge.

The hope almost vanished when she used inseeing on the house.

All the protection spells had been replaced by a sticky-looking purple slime. It glistened on the slates of the roof, ran slowly down the walls and dripped from the guttering, drawing itself out into long strands.

Dido's first impulse was to cast a cleaning spell – something with plenty of detergent and disinfectant in it – but she checked herself. It would be a waste of energy. The goo was gross but harmless, a by–product of Light and Shadow Magic clashing and cancelling each other out.

Round One to you, Miss M, thought Dido.

Still inseeing, she crept around the side of the house and tried the back door. It was locked. Dido could have used an unlocking spell, but again it would take up energy that she might need later. She glanced down the garden, wondering if her parents had stashed a spare key in the sanctuary, and gasped.

The sanctuary had been slimed too. It was a mean thing to do, sheer vandalism, and Dido was appalled. The Nesbit family's most private place had been desecrated.

A wave of black fury surged through Dido, and expressed itself in a spell that was half giant, hobnailed boot and half battering-ram.

The back door silently exploded into slivers of wood and granules of glass. The empty hinges dropped on to the kitchen floor. The kitchen looked as though a bomb had hit it, which it had.

Dido crossed the threshold, her feet scrunching on the remains of the door, and went into the hall. The lounge door was open, and Miss Morgan's voice emerged from it.

'Ah, there you are, Dido! Do come in.'

Dido entered the lounge.

Miss Morgan was standing in the centre of the room. Dido's parents were on the sofa, sitting stiffly upright, their faces and eyes expressionless.

'Mum, Dad – are you OK?' said Dido.

There was no response.

Dido glared at Miss Morgan.

'What have you done to them?' she demanded.

Miss Morgan beamed.

'They've been relocated,' she said. 'Their bodies remain in this world, but their spirits have been sent somewhere else.'

'Where?'

'You'll find out soon enough.'

'And what about Cosmo?'

'Your familiar knows a thing or two, doesn't she?' Miss Morgan said with reluctant admiration. 'She was too quick for me. She's probably hiding somewhere. It isn't important. I'll find her after I've dealt with you and your parents.'

It was weird. This was the same Miss Morgan who'd taught Dido Drama in Year Seven, one of the most inspiring and popular teachers at Prince Arthur's Comp. It was difficult for Dido to believe that she'd been completely taken over by evil.

There has to be something of the real Miss Morgan left, thought Dido. She said, 'You don't have to do this. There's another way. Bring Mum and Dad back and we can talk about it.'

Miss Morgan laughed.

'Appealing to my better nature isn't going to work, Dido,' she said. 'If you went down on your knees and begged me, I might find it amusing, but it wouldn't stop me. My instructions are quite specific. You're to be annihilated.'

'Instructions? Whose instructions?'

Miss Morgan regarded Dido as if she were a young child who'd asked a stupid question.

'Does it really matter, Dido? Soon, nothing will matter to you any more. You'll have no problems, no anxieties, no decisions to make, just eternal peace and oblivion. It's very appealing, in a way. And I think it's time to begin, don't you?'

The light flickered, as though Dido had blinked, and the lounge wasn't there. The change was so rapid that Dido didn't feel a thing. One instant she was at home, the next she was in another place, in a narrow ravine that was littered with boulders, enclosed by sheer cliffs of black rock. The rock was shiny, reflecting the gloomy light in shades of grey, and looked as if it had once been liquid. Its surface was whorled and rippled, and ridged puddles stood where the walls and floor met. At one end a rock fall was close by, a tumble of dark blocks with sharp edges. At the other end, the ravine turned left. Dido wondered where it led and made her way towards the bend. Steadying herself to clamber over a boulder, she put both hands on its surface and felt it cold and warm against her skin. The stone was thawing and freezing at the same time.

Neither one thing, nor the other, Dido thought. The perfect spot for a showdown with a Shadowmaster.

Dido rounded the corner, and what she saw on the other side tore a cry of despair from her. The sides of the ravine echoed and re-echoed her cry until the sound fluttered like birds.

Two shapes were embedded in the stone – two

glossy statues; one male, one female – Mum and Dad.

A hard lump swelled in Dido's throat and tears welled in her eyes.

'I might as well give up,' she whispered. 'If Miss Morgan can do this to Mum and Dad, what chance do I stand?'

It was the worst moment of Dido's life, and the misery of it was crushing. She'd got involved with Shadow Magic, managed to defeat a Shadowmaster, and it had made her cocky. Now it seemed to have been beginner's luck. Mum and Dad had warned her, but Dido hadn't listened, and they were all suffering because of it.

Dido didn't often feel like a kid, but suddenly being going-on thirteen didn't seem nearly as grown up as she'd thought. She'd messed up Big Time.

Something intruded on her grief, not so much a sound as a faint pressure in her head. Dido concentrated on it with inseeing and heard Mum's voice, coming from far away.

'No, Dido, you haven't failed. Look in our eyes.'

Dido frowned, suspecting a trap.

'Mum?' she said. 'Is that you?'

'Look in our eyes!'

Dido almost raised a smile. Mum's tone was the

same as when she was being Mrs Nesbit, Deputy Head. It was definitely her.

Dido peered closely at the statues and saw nothing. Their eyes were blank.

'Deeper!' Mum urged.

Dido looked again, and caught sight of a white fleck in her mother's right eye, a glimmer. Dido bobbed her head to make sure that it wasn't a reflection, and the glimmer stayed fixed. There was a similar fleck in her father's right eye, but it was coloured pink.

'Witch lights!' Dido murmured.

She made her own witch light, her best yet, a deep, buttery yellow that shone clearly. Mum's voice sounded louder, and she could hear Dad too.

'Cast an unlocking spell,' said Mum.

'No, Dido,' Dad said. 'Use a becoming spell.'

'But we haven't taught her any becoming spells,' protested Mum.

'Dido doesn't need to be taught, the spell's already inside her. Find it, Dido.'

Instead, Dido let the spell find her. She imagined herself on an enormous helter-skelter, thousands of metres high, then she took away the slide and the tower, and she was spiralling downwards.

The spell developed at the hub of the spiral, and it was powerful. Dido saw newborn colts struggling upright on shaky legs, fronds of fern bursting their way through tarmac, the beaks of chicks piercing the shells that encased them. The life in them all was a force that couldn't be held back.

The statues split. The stone turned to a powder that was finer than flour. Mum and Dad stepped out of the cliff, on to the floor of the ravine.

The Nesbits hugged. The hug felt like the safest place that Dido had ever been, even though she knew that it was flimsier than wet tissue paper.

Mum said, 'Alice Morgan—'

'Is a Shadowmaster. I know,' said Dido. 'She's the one who set off the fire alarms at school.'

'She took us completely by surprise,' said Dad. 'We were overwhelmed.'

'My guess is that she's getting ready to come here after us, but she can't overwhelm the three of us,' Dido said defiantly. 'We're going to take her apart.'

'No,' said Mum. 'She's in the grip of Shadow Magic, and she's not really responsible for her actions. We mustn't harm her.'

Dido backed out of the hug and stared at her mother in disbelief.

'She wants to kill us, Mum!' she said.

'The Shadow Magic wants to kill us, not Alice.'

'Well, excuse me, but either way we wind up dead, don't we?'

'Steady!' said Dad. 'If you two would co-operate instead of arguing, we might get out of this. Dido will do what has to be done. We need her help, Faye.'

'Me – help you?' said Dido.

'Yes,' Dad said. 'You're stronger than the two of us put together, Dido. I thought you knew.'

'I didn't.'

'Then get used to the idea – fast.'

But there was no time to get used to anything. Dido's thumbs began to itch, and she knew that trouble was on its way.

'Miss Morgan's here,' she said.

Instinctively, the Nesbits stood side by side, with Dido in between Mum and Dad.

Ten metres ahead, a violet mist rose from a fissure in the floor. The mist was thin at first, wisps that curled playfully, then it thickened, rushing out of the ground like smoke from the fuse of a firework. There was a shape inside the mist, a shape that shook its head, and lashed its tail, and screeched harshly, and rumbled forwards.

The thing was part dragon and part tank, rolling along on scaled tracks. Curved spines protruded from the dragon's back, and a pair of tiny wings lay folded between its shoulders. The head was wedge-shaped, snake-like, with cunning yellow eyes and a mouth filled with fangs like bone icicles. The dragon extended its thick purple tongue, tasting the scent in the air. It saw the Nesbits and screeched again, drawing back its head.

Common sense told Dido to give in to her terror and run, but her magic made her shout, 'Shield!'

Dad hummed a note. Mum and Dido joined in, their three voices harmonising.

A metal grille rolled down in front of the Nesbits, just as a jet of electric-blue fire roared from the dragon's gaping jaws. The flames splashed back from the bars of the grille, and Dido felt a blast of heat singe her hair.

The flames lasted less than half a minute, but left the grille blackened. The cooling metal chinked and tinkled.

The dragon advanced at full tilt, crashing into the bars, thrashing them with its tail, seizing them in its jaws. The bars groaned and buckled.

Holding the grille in place took a lot of effort. Dad's teeth were tight shut, and Mum's face was ashen. Dido felt like a clenched hand in an arm-wrestling contest.

'We can't keep this up forever,' Dad said hoarsely. 'Dido, use your Shadow Magic!'

Dido was so shocked that she almost lost her hold on the shielding spell.

'My Shadow Magic?' she squeaked.

'No more games, Dido,' said Dad. 'We know what you've been doing.'

'But how?'

'Later,' said Dad. 'For now, just show us what you can do.'

Unfortunately, Dido didn't see how she could do anything.

'I can't!' she groaned. 'I can't use Light Magic and Shadow Magic at the same time, and if I let go of the shield—'

In a low voice, Mum said, 'Have faith in yourself, Dido. You can do anything.'

Dido thought of her Light side – the figure of the Goddess in the sanctuary, her witch light, the horns of the new moon in the night sky. Then she pictured her Shadow side, the panther she had seen drinking from the pool in the heart of her magic. The panther bared its teeth in a snarl.

A spell boiled up from within Dido and darted out of her eyes, rearing and snorting behind the dragon. The spell appeared as a black unicorn the size of a shire horse. Its eyes glittered red, its long tapered horn was the colour of copper. The unicorn stamped its hooves, sending out cascades of white-hot sparks.

The dragon wheeled around and breathed fire. The unicorn vaulted over the dragon, and as it landed, swung its head to tear a long gash in the scaly flank. Blood oozed out, glowing orange-red, like volcanic lava. The dragon writhed, its tank tracks squealing.

The unicorn kicked the dragon's head with its back hooves, shattering teeth and bone. It kicked again, and again, and again.

'Stop it!' said Mum.

'I can't,' Dido said. She was horrified by the unicorn's savagery. It was enjoying the attack, relishing its enemy's agony. It wouldn't stop until it had sunk its horn into the dragon's heart.

Words Dido hadn't heard before forced their way past her lips, and she spoke in a language she didn't understand.

'A bethi breeg na tharl!'

The grille crashed into a heap of twisted metal. The unicorn melted into shadows. The dragon withered and contracted into Miss Morgan, prone on the dark rock, with her face turned to one side. A witch light hung over her, wavering uncertainly, the same witch light that Dido had seen outside the Sanctuary.

Her magic must have been trying to reach out to the Goddess, Dido thought, but Spelkor got to her first.

'Go into the light,' said Dad.

'Why would we want anything to do with her light?' Dido asked.

'Because it's the way home.'

Dido joined her parents in inseeing, and it felt even closer than their hug. Mum was bright and quick, funny and solemn. Dad was patient, steady and calm. Dido wondered how she felt to them.

The witch light brightened until Dido couldn't look at it. Its radiance beamed through her skin, illuminating every cell in her body. A wind made of light blew into her face.

And the light went out.

Dido was in the lounge, standing next to Dad.

Mum had her arms around Miss Morgan, who was crying.

'What's going on?' Miss Morgan sobbed. 'What am I doing here?'

'It's all right,' said Mum. 'You're going to be all right – we all are.'

Dad nudged Dido with his elbow and said, 'Shall we go and put the kettle on?'

'Er, we might have to tidy up the kitchen first.'

Dad rolled his eyes.

'Let's get it sorted then,' he said.

Before they got to the kitchen, Dido and Dad were interrupted by Cosmo. She came bounding down the stairs, chattering busily. She was telling Dido and her parents off, asking them what they thought they were doing swanning off without a word, getting up to who-knew-what. Cosmo had been frantic. They hadn't let her know, no one had sent her a message—

'Yeah, yeah, I hear you,' Dido said. 'There's no need to get your knicks in a knot, we're all safe.'

Cosmo said something else.

'Let me guess,' said Dad. 'That was Cat for – "In that case, why doesn't someone feed me"?'

'Right,' Dido said.

21
The Covening

It took ages to sort out the kitchen. Dad had to pay emergency rates for someone to fit a new back door, and when that was fixed, there was the de-sliming of the house and the sanctuary to see to. It would have been easier with Mum's help, but she'd taken Miss Morgan home, saying that Miss Morgan was too shaken up to drive, so Dido and Dad copped the lot. It was gone seven before they finished, and there was still no sign of Mum.

Dad collapsed on to the sofa in the lounge. Dido sprawled in an armchair.

'Should we do something about dinner?' Dad said.

'I'm too knackered to move,' said Dido. 'How about phoning for a pizza when Mum gets back?'

'Sounds good to me.' Dad scratched the stubble on his chin, wriggled around and cleared his throat, like he had something to tell Dido, but wasn't sure how to go about it. 'I'm proud of you,' he said finally. 'What you did earlier on was...well, incredible is the only word that comes close.'

'You and Mum did your bit too.'

Dad shrugged off the compliment with a modest smile.

Dido said, 'Dad, it's "later".'

'Meaning?'

'Meaning that when I asked you how you and Mum knew about my Shadow Magic, you said, "later", so are you going to tell me or not?'

Dido had obviously put Dad in an awkward position, because there was more scratching, wriggling and coughing.

'We've always known,' he said. 'We even helped you along from time to time.'

'You did?'

'Why d'you think we bought you all those books of fairy tales when you were little?'

'But you and Mum always said—'

'What all Light Witches say to their children – stay away from Shadow Magic – but we knew you wouldn't.'

'How come?'

'Because you're wayward, wilful and you always manage to get your own way.'

'Flattery isn't going to put me off,' said Dido. 'That's not the real reason, is it?'

'No,' Dad confessed. 'It was partly that thing where kids always do what their parent tell them not to, and partly because we were told not to interfere.'

'By?'

'The Goddess.'

The room went very still.

'You spoke to the Goddess?' Dido said, awed.

'She spoke to us through our witch spirits. She told us to let you develop your own relationship with Shadow Magic – and it certainly paid off today, didn't it?'

Dido was so tired that she found it hard to follow what Dad was saying.

'Wait up a minute,' she said. 'Let's get this straight, everybody has a Shadow side, don't they?'

'Not like yours, and most Light Witches keep their Shadow selves under wraps.'

'So why did the Goddess tell you to leave me alone – am I different or something?'

'I'm not supposed to say anything until your Covening.'

'Then break the rules.'

Dad sighed.

'It's not that easy, Dido,' he said. 'Your mother and I gave the Goddess our word, and we can't go back on it.'

And, short of using a persuasion spell on Dad, which even Dido wouldn't stoop to, that was all she could get out of him. His silence was maddening, but Dido understood the reason for it. A promise was a promise after all, especially a promise made to the Goddess.

Mum came in at half seven, barely able to keep her eyes open.

'How's Miss Morgan?' Dido asked.

'Getting there,' said Mum. 'Though what we found in her flat didn't help.'

'What did you find?'

'A cat, or rather, the remains of a cat. It must have been dead for weeks.'

Dido shuddered, then said, 'What's going to happen to Miss Morgan now?'

Mum put a hand up to her mouth to stifle a yawn.

'The Shadow Magic's left her,' she said. 'She doesn't remember much about it, which is probably just as well, but her Light side is intact. I'm going to give her lessons in how to be a Light Witch, once a week, after school. You can help me, if you like.'

'Excuse me?' said Dido. 'Me – teach a teacher? I don't think so.'

On Saturday morning Dido did the supermarket run with her parents, not that she enjoyed supermarket shopping, but the togetherness the Nesbits had shared in the ravine was still working.

After lunch, Mum and Dad went down to the sanctuary to meditate, and Dido caught the bus into town. She wasn't sure if any of her friends would be waiting for her, and was pleased to find Philippa seated on a bench near the statue of Queen Victoria. Philippa looked solemn, and Dido soon discovered why.

'I talked to Dad about Mum last night,' she said.

'And?'

'He told me the truth about Mum's accident. She was walking out on us. She had this thing with her boss, and she told Dad about it, and then she left. Dad said she'd been drinking.'

'Why didn't he tell you before?'

'First he had trouble accepting that she'd found someone else, then I started to turn her into some kind of saint and—' Philippa huffed. 'Who knows why grown-ups do the things they do? I wasn't surprised when he told me. It was like I already knew it, but I didn't want to let myself know that I knew. I was in thingummy.'

'Denial?'

'That's the one,' Philippa said. 'I took all my resentment out on Alison. I've been such an idiot, Dido.'

'You'll live,' said Dido. 'Hey, is Ollie coming this afternoon?'

'Yeah. He rang for a chat this morning and said he was.'

Ollie hardly ever rang Dido, and once again Dido felt a twinge of jealousy. It seemed that not all her feelings about Philippa had been down to the distractor.

'It's a shame Scott can't get together with us on Saturdays, isn't it?' Philippa said.

'Uh huh. He's tied up at home – but then he would be, wouldn't he?'

'Why?'

'Tied up? Escapology?'

Philippa groaned, which was all the joke deserved.

'D'you think Scott's good-looking?' she said.

'I suppose.'

'I do. I reckon Scott's going to be pretty tasty in a year or two.'

'How about Ollie?'

Philippa shrugged, and wrinkled her nose.

'Ollie is OK, if you like redheads,' she said. 'He's too good a mate to be a boyfriend.'

'I guess,' said Dido.

Ollie emerged from the crowds on the other side of the road, saw Dido and Philippa, smiled and waved.

Dido waved back, hoping that Philippa was wrong. Mate or not, Ollie would make an ideal boyfriend.

Dido's thirteenth birthday fell on a Sunday. Dad cooked her favourite breakfast, pancakes with maple syrup, and she opened the cards that had arrived earlier in the week. On the front of the largest and most colourful card was a drawing of a girl dancing through swirls of musical notes, with WILD TEEN printed above her in gold letters. The message inside read, YOU ARE THE BEST! and it was signed by Scott, Philippa and Ollie.

After she'd looked through all her cards, Mum and Dad gave Dido her presents, the new jeans and the CD that she'd asked for, and a surprise present wrapped in plain brown paper. Inside the wrapping was a spirit-mirror, a crystal ball on a black wooden stand. Dido was so delighted that she couldn't think what to say.

'Don't you like it?' Mum asked anxiously.

'I love it to bits!' said Dido.

'Better not,' Dad advised. 'Remember the spirit-mirror you broke last year?'

'I'll be careful with this one,' Dido promised.

'You'll need your own spirit-mirror now that you're an adult witch,' said Dad. 'From today on, you'll be studying magic by yourself. Your mother and I will still give you advice, of course.'

'Whether I ask for it or not?' Dido said.

Dad laughed. 'I expect so.'

Despite his laughter, Dad seemed a little sad – Mum too. Dido supposed it was because her becoming an adult witch was making them feel old, but she was wrong. Her parents were sad for a different reason, and it wasn't long before Dido found out what the reason was.

*

The Covening was held at dusk. Dido, Mum, Dad and Cosmo went down the back garden to the sanctuary. After asking the Goddess's permission for Dad to enter – a tradition that stretched back to the time when Light Witches had been exclusively female – they went inside.

Mum lit a candle, set it on the floor, then fetched an empty tumbler, a tumbler of water and a flint, lined them up and sat cross-legged behind them. Dad sat beside her and Cosmo sat beside Dad. They all faced Dido.

'Should I sit down too?' she said.

'It's up to you,' said Dad.

Dido felt a little awkward about looking down on her parents, and sat.

Mum pointed at the candle, the tumblers and the flint.

'Fire, air, water and earth,' she said. 'The air is in our breathing, the earth is in our flesh and bones, fire and water run in our blood.'

'We follow the Light,' said Dad. 'The sun, and the moon, and the stars. Are you a follower of the Light?'

'Yes,' said Dido.

The candle glowed brighter, sharpening the shadows in the sanctuary.

'The Light holds back the darkness, but the darkness is still there,' said Mum. 'In the earth, beneath the stone, between the stars. Hold the Light in your heart.'

'Keep it there always,' Dad said.

'I will,' said Dido.

The glow from the candle spread to the tumblers, making them quiver like flames. The flint shone glossily.

'Accept the Light,' said Mum.

'I do,' Dido said.

Light and shadows filled her eyes and flowed through her, fusing together until she felt at one with the twilight gathering outside.

'Welcome to the Light,' Mum and Dad chorused.

Dido accepted a kiss of greeting from both her parents, then crouched on the floor so that she could touch noses with Cosmo. Mum and Dad seemed tense, and Dido tried to lighten the atmosphere.

'Well that went OK, didn't it?' she said.

Dad took something down from a shelf.

'Now that your Covening is over, we've got something to tell you, Dido,' he said. His tone of voice suggested that it wasn't something cheerful.

'Oh?' Dido said apprehensively.

Dad handed Dido a transparent document folder and said, 'Read that.'

Inside the folder was a single sheet of ancient parchment. The edges of the sheet were ragged and the parchment was cracked, and stained with grease. Someone had written on it, long enough ago to have used a quill pen by the look of it, and the ink had faded. Dido had to tilt the wallet to catch the light to make out some of the words.

In the Beginning was the Twilight, and the Lady and her Lord wrought great works of Magic. But Lord Spelkor grew envious of his Lady's power, and strove to rule over all. He stole the Shadow from the Twilight and took it for his own. Then Light came to the World, he tried to steal that also. There was war in the Heavens, and on the Earth, and in the Oceans. The Earth spewed fire and brought forth great mountains. But the Light prevailed. Lord Spelkor was cast down into the bowels of the Hill of Caledor, and bound there with mighty spells. And there he shall remain until the Time of the Stars, when he will come forth to make a new World, and the Old Ways will be no more.

'Is the Lady the Goddess?' said Dido.

Mum nodded.

'She and Spelkor were a couple? Crazy stuff! What's it got to do with me?'

'Everything,' Mum said. 'The Hill of Caledor is Stanstowe Hill. It's Spelkor's prison. When you were conceived, the Goddess gave you the spirit of a great Twilight Witch, perhaps the greatest witch who ever lived, Lilil. When the Time of the Stars comes, Spelkor will be free—'

Dido was way ahead of her mother.

'And I have to fight him, right?' she said.

She felt as though her stomach had dropped into her shoes.

'No one knows what chaos and ruin Spelkor will cause,' said Dad. 'But millions of people may suffer if he isn't stopped, and you're the only one who has a chance of stopping him.'

Dido was numb.

'How big a chance?' she said. 'And when is this Time of the Stars going to be?'

'No one knows that either,' said Dad. 'It could be tomorrow, or in twenty years from now. As for your chances, you've already beaten Spelkor twice.'

'Twice?'

'Alice Morgan and Hugh Purdey,' said Mum.

'You knew about Mr Purdey?'

Mum nodded.

'That was harder than yesterday,' she said. 'You were up against your first Shadowmaster, and I couldn't do anything to help you. I couldn't even tell you about it.'

'OK, so I've defeated Spelkor twice,' said Dido, 'but both times he was chained down. How strong will he be when he's free?'

Neither Mum nor Dad replied.

There was more talk, more explanations. By the time Dido went to bed, everything her parents told her was spinning round and round in her head, and she couldn't sleep. She opened the bedroom curtains, sat on top of the duvet and gazed at the night, stroking Cosmo. Doubts tormented her, and she spoke the worst doubt out loud.

'What if I can't hack it, Coz? What if I screw up and—'

Cosmo purred the Cat equivalent of, 'Count your blessings, kid!'

So Dido took Cosmo's advice, and counted her blessings. There turned out to be more than she'd expected. She had loving parents, a wise and faithful familiar, good friends that she could trust, Lilil and, most importantly of all, the Goddess was on her side.

Dido fixed her eyes on the half moon that was sailing above the rooftops.

'Are you there?' she whispered. 'Are you watching over me? Are you going to help me get through this?'

A falling meteorite drew a bright line in the sky, so short-lived that it was there and gone in the same instant.

Dido took it as a yes.

Other Red Apples to get your teeth into.

Chris d'Lacey

David soon discovers the dragons when he moves in with Liz and Lucy. The pottery models fill up every spare space in the house!

Only when David is given his own special dragon does he begin to unlock their mysterious secrets and to discover the fire within.

Pat Moon

Loads of secret stuff about BOYS, worry bugs, babies, enemies, etcetera, etcetera. Snoopers will be savaged by Twinkle (warrior-princess guinea pig).

Do Not Read This Book was shortlisted for the Sheffield Book Award

More Orchard Red Apples

The Fire Within	Chris d'Lacey	1 84121 533 3
The Salt Pirates of Skegness	Chris d'Lacey	1 84121 539 2
The Poltergoose	Michael Lawrence	1 86039 836 7
The Killer Underpants	Michael Lawrence	1 84121 713 1
The Toilet of Doom	Michael Lawrence	1 84121 752 2
Maggot Pie	Michael Lawrence	1 84121 756 5
Do Not Read This Book	Pat Moon	1 84121 435 3
Do Not Read Any Further	Pat Moon	1 84121 456 6
How to Eat Fried Worms	Thomas Rockwell	1 84362 206 8
How to Get Fabulously Rich	Thomas Rockwell	1 84362 207 6
How to Fight a Girl	Thomas Rockwell	1 84362 208 4

All books priced at £4.99

Orchard Red Apples are available from all good bookshops,
or can be ordered direct from the publisher: Orchard Books,
PO BOX 29, Douglas IM99 1BQ
Credit card orders please telephone 01624 836000
or fax 01624 837033 or visit our Internet site: www.wattspub.co.uk
or e-mail: bookshop@enterprise.net for details.

To order please quote title, author and ISBN
and your full name and address.
Cheques and postal orders should be made payable to 'Bookpost plc.'
Postage and packing is FREE within the UK
(overseas customers should add £1.00 per book).

Prices and availability are subject to change.